Radio Sunrise

Anietie Isong

JACARANDA

First published in Great Britain 2017 by
Jacaranda Books Art Music Ltd
Unit 304 Metal Box Factory
30 Great Guildford Street,
London SE1 0HS
www.jacarandabooksartmusic.co.uk

ISBN: 978-1-909762-37-4
eISBN: 978-1-909762-38-1

Printed and bound in India by Imprint Digital
48 Thellusson Way, Penn Heights,
Rickmansworth, Herts WD3 8RQ

To my parents

Hold a true friend with both hands.
—Nigerian proverb

Chapter 1

On a hot July afternoon, two men were weeping near The Lord Is My Shepherd Foods canteen. One of them was wearing an adire and the other a tight T-shirt with "Big Man" inscribed in huge letters across the front.

"He touched me," the man in the T-shirt cried. "He touched me."

"I didn't do it," the other man protested. "I swear to God, it wasn't me!"

A crowd had gathered. I took out my voice recorder, a miniature thing, only slightly bigger than my index finger. As a journalist, it was imperative I went everywhere with this tool. In Lagos, news could break at any time. I recognised a few faces in the crowd, some of whom were The Lord Is My Shepherd Foods customers.

"He has taken my manhood away o!" the man in the T-shirt howled.

It was another missing penis case. People said that a mere touch from an evil hand could make a penis vanish. Just like that! One minute a man was a man and the next moment his manhood was gone. They said the missing organ often became a money-maker in a spiritualist's shrine. Some Lagos publications stoked the rumour with their sensational headlines: "MAN'S PENIS DISAPPEARS INTO THIN AIR"; "FEAR IN THE CITY: TWENTY PENISES MISSING";

"BEWARE: PENIS SNATCHERS ON THE PROWL".

"I did not do it," the accused man suddenly protested.

"Who did it?" a trader yelled. "You are one of these evil people. God has arrested you today. Instead of you finding a good job, you want to spoil other people's business. God has caught you today!"

Someone suggested loudly that both men should be taken to the police.

"Police?" another retorted. "Why bother with them? We have eyes. And we have seen what has happened. We have the means to carry out judgement ourselves. We will teach this man sense here. We will teach him to respect other people's sacred property."

I raised my voice recorder in order to capture every sound. Should I worry about what this crowd could do? I knew about jungle justice. I had seen it many times in the city. Last year, in the suburb of Lagos, I saw angry traders set fire to a man who had stolen fresh meat from the butchers. The police arrived at the scene a minute too late. For many days, I couldn't eat beef. Just a whiff of cooked meat would force me to gag at the memory of the thief's charred face and dismembered arm. I wondered if a similar fate would befall the penis snatcher. Would someone save him from the fury of the mob?

"What will I do now?" the victim lamented. "How can I perform my manly duties? I just got married three weeks ago. My wife is yet to be pregnant, you know."

The victim looked quite young, too young to be a husband, I thought, but then I remembered my neighbour, the twenty-year-old carpenter who had three wives.

A man in a green uniform pushed his way through the crowd to the front. People turned, took a quick look at him and immediately gave way to the power of a uniform.

"Hold on, gentleman and ladies," the uniformed man suddenly shouted. "Let us not get carried away. I have seen a lot of things since I have been working in this area. I have seen the good; I have seen the bad. I want us to ascertain the correct circumstances here. Let this man, this victim of missing penis prove to us that his organ has vanished. Let him undress."

"The official speaks well," some people were murmuring; "It is good to check these things." More people joined the crowd. I could see the waitress from The Lord Is My Shepherd Foods, the light-skinned girl who always wore an oil-stained apron. My barber was there too and the guy who sold phone recharge cards by the entrance to my radio station.

"Haba, officer," someone called out, "how can a man undress in the street?"

The official smiled. "Why not? He has nothing to hide in those trousers. We must determine if all his equipment has disappeared. It might be only the scrotum that has vanished. Before we administer judgment, let us analyse the whole situation. Doesn't that make sense?"

I desperately wanted to say something. I wanted the man in the uniform to stop the crowd before they went too far, but I pushed the words down. It was my duty as a journalist not to influence people. My role was to report the event as it happened and let the good people of Lagos relish whatever they chose to. That was it. Nothing more.

Someone said it made a lot of sense for the man to undress.

"I am not undressing," the man protested, "at least not here. Let us go somewhere else, anywhere but here."

"Oh but yes, you will undress here," the uniformed man insisted.

I had covered many bizarre events in Lagos. I was there at Bar Beach when a woman in a white garment claimed to have turned into a bird. I was at Ikoyi Cemetery when a war veteran woke up two minutes before his coffin was lowered to the grave. That story made the network news at 4 in the afternoon and I received a letter of commendation directly from the Director of News. I was determined to add the penis-snatching saga to my list of bizarre news stories.

I pushed my way to the front just in time to see the victim's trousers being yanked off. The man wore nothing underneath and his manhood peered at the crowd. A woman's shriek began the uproarious response. I didn't know how the victim managed to break away from the crowd so suddenly, but he did. He was a fast runner, that man. People started fighting, pushing and screaming:

"Stupid man! God punish you!"

"Don't let him get away. Catch him!"

"We must teach you never to deceive people."

I had never really been a good runner. I did very little sport, to be honest. I wasn't made for endurance or for speed, so I didn't bother to join the race. I left it for the notorious street sprinters, those hawkers who would run kilometres to sell their groundnuts and handkerchiefs to motorists.

They got him after a short chase and dragged him back to where the mob waited.

"I want to know why you wrongly accused this man," someone called out. "I think everyone here wants to know."

"Yes, we want to know," another agreed. "We would have killed an innocent man, if not for the kind uniformed man in our midst."

"We shouldn't waste time on this matter," someone bellowed. "Let's get on with it."

"Yes!" the crowd screamed.

The barber brought an old tyre, a young man fetched a can

of petrol and I recorded all the sounds: all the cries and pleas. I saw a man produce a box of matches. Cars sped past. I waited, recording everything.

"Ladies and gentlemen," the uniformed man was shouting over the top of the baying crowd, "let's be rational about this. Do not take the law into your own hands. I beg of you, good people of Lagos, let us not set fire to this man. Let us hear his side of the story."

The man's pleas only inflamed the mob further. When someone opened the can of petrol, those around him cheered. I backed away to the edge of the mass of people, which is how I saw the truck, when few others did. Few people were aware of the truck driver losing his struggle to control the steering, while his vehicle swerved wildly towards the centre of the crowd. Finally, my tongue loosened. I screamed and screamed.

"Thank God the truck scattered the crowd and no one died," Yetunde said, when I narrated the incident to her at my flat. "That is why I tell you to stay away from The Lord Is My Shepherd Foods. That restaurateur is evil."

I immediately regretted telling her the story. Everyone knew Mama Joe, a retired nurse, managed the eatery. Poor woman! Some people cooked up unsavoury tales about her and her business. They said she sprinkled magical herbs by her door, so as to increase the number of visitors to the restaurant. They said her husband was a chief herbalist who specialised in making assorted concoctions for politicians and businessmen. My sweetheart, Yetunde, swallowed these stories whole. Me, I didn't buy such tales. I loved food. Good and affordable food. At The Lord Is My Shepherd Foods, there was plenty of that: goat head pepper soup, cow tail stew, fried snail, Jollof rice. The restaurant was situated only three buildings away from Radio Sunrise.

I wasn't in the mood to argue with Yetunde so I steered the conversation towards fashion: I told her I liked her new dress. She beamed. The dress was from Beautiful Selections, a boutique in Yaba whose slogan was "We go the extra mile." The shop specialised in secondhand clothes and indeed the proprietor—the gigantic Mr Nwachukwu—always went the extra mile to wash and iron the garments, making them smell and look as new as possible. Last week, after dinner, Yetunde had proudly displayed the newly-introduced loyalty card— *Beautiful Card*, a small thing made from recycled paper. Her patronage of Beautiful Selections had nothing to do with money, she had made it clear to me from the beginning, when we had started dating. Because the clothes were imported from the United Kingdom, Yetunde believed that Cheryl Cole or some other celebrity may have been the original owners of these dresses. It was the thought of sharing clothes with the famous that made her frequent Mr Nwachukwu's business.

"The dress really looks perfect on you," I said.

"Really?" Yetunde exclaimed.

"Yes."

She was pleased. "Let me dance for you."

Yetunde always expressed her happiness through dance. Slowly, she lifted one arm, then the other. She swayed first to the left, then to the right. Smiling, she whirled through a series of pirouettes.

"Anyone who sings well and dances well is well educated," Yetunde said. "My darling, are you well educated?"

"I am well educated," I replied. "I dance in my heart."

She laughed. "Let me give you some dance tips."

Her soft hands clasped mine. I rose feebly to my feet. I hated those tutorials. Some people, I believed, were born to dance. Others were born to be spectators, to clap and encourage the dancer when necessary. I belonged to the latter category of people. And although I tried to move to the beat of the song blaring from the CD player, although I tried to wriggle like her, it was no use. It was as if a grinding stone had been tied to my ankles. But I was not really bothered. I knew the dance was just a prelude to lovemaking.

"Dance, my darling," Yetunde urged.

My hands eventually did the dancing. My fingers danced on her face. They danced on her neck and down to her chest. They danced lower and lower.

My eyes lingered on my lover's body. She was still naked.

"I'll go prepare your meal," she announced, as she threw on a robe and walked towards the kitchen.

I followed her. I had every reason to be thankful—I had a beautiful lady who could cook all sorts of meals, from egusi to moi moi. She liked to shop in the market in Lagos Island, where she said the prices were great and she could find everything from red onions to octopus. I could not stand that market. I could not stand the traders' indulgent calls. I could not stand the large flies that hovered around the refuse dump at the entrance to the market. Everything Yetunde touched in the kitchen was transformed. The Eagle gas cooker, which I had thought was on its last legs, had suddenly come alive after Yetunde gave it a good clean. Whenever Yetunde stayed for a few days at my flat, she always cooked two different pots of stew. The one made with palm oil and lots of pepper was the sort that could make a tongue bleed. The other pot of stew, made with groundnut oil and less pepper, was milder. My stomach always growled whenever I had too much spice.

I watched her slice the plantain and lower it gently into

the simmering vegetable oil. She added green pepper to the fish. Then, she started chopping the tomatoes in tiny pieces. Yetunde said that she spent the entire day looking for the right tomatoes to buy at the market. "Do you know that some restaurants in Lagos use rotten tomatoes?" she asked me. I didn't want to think of rotten food. My stomach longed only for the fried plantain and fish stew being prepared under my gaze. I licked my lips a thousand times before the food was ready.

As we ate Yetunde told me about a new doctor at her hospital. She had heard talk of the man's flirtatious ways, that he did it with any woman who came his way: the nurses, fellow doctors and even the maids who cleaned the wards.

"And he is a married man!" she spat. "You should see his wife. She looks like a model. What do you men want? Why can't you ever be satisfied with a good woman? Tell me, Ifiok. I want to know."

Luckily, a call from my mother saved me from a very difficult explanation.

"How are you?" my mum asked. Before I could answer, she launched into a long story.

"Chief Edem, your father's second cousin, has built a new borehole for the community. And it's completely free. Can you imagine that? Free water to everybody! God will bless him a million times. He has..."

My parents lived in Ibok, my hometown, in the Niger Delta of Nigeria. Whenever my mother called, she always had something to say: a distant relative had built a new house or someone had given birth. I listened attentively to these stories. I was expected to do so.

When I hung up, Yetunde was engrossed in the Mexican soap opera on TV.

Chapter 2

"Oga, you will get your car first thing on Saturday morning," Solomon had told me with that sweet tongue of his.

Solomon, the proprietor of The Heavenly Bread Mechanic Workshop had promised to fix the faulty starter of my car. Sometimes, I called him Engineer Solomon, even though I knew he was not a qualified engineer. He had not even smelt the backyard of an engineering school. Word went round that he had learnt to repair cars somewhere in the eastern part of the country, in a village where everyone could fix cars and motorcycles.

And despite swearing a thousand times, he failed to deliver. I had to go to work by bus. I could have taken the taxi motorcycle, which was ten times faster, but those riders had no respect for lives. People said that every morning when they woke up, they rinsed their mouths with the local gin. The drink made them think they were birds. It made them want to fly on Third Mainland Bridge. "They will drive you to hell, these motorcyclists," Yetunde warned.

The bus was full but I managed to get a seat near the front, sandwiched between a woman in black and a man in a grey suit. I wiped my face with a white handkerchief and sat back to enjoy the ride. The bus was part of a government mass transit scheme, launched amid much fanfare on Workers Day. The market women had sung many songs, praising the governor for giving the masses the vehicles. "Our governor is a man of the masses; see, he has given us our own air-conditioned bus!" they sang. I did a story about the buses, reporting on the numbered seats and the sign on the door saying, "Please, Don't Mess in this Bus."

As the bus puffed along, my eyes darted across the road to the face of a beggar. He was surrounded by the paraphernalia of his trade: a sordid plate, a walking stick, an old umbrella. Perhaps I could weave a story around the beggar for my radio drama, I thought to myself. Apart from my reporting duties, I was also the current producer of a popular radio drama called *The River* on Radio Sunrise.

"I greet you, distinguished ladies and gentlemen," a man suddenly shouted inside the bus. "Forgive me for otherwise intruding, but what I am about to reveal to you is of utmost importance and urgency. I urge you, good people in this bus, to give me your attention."

I turned and looked at the man, who was armed with a black bag. Though I couldn't see his face clearly, I knew the man's intent. Many years ago, the government agency for food and drugs had declared that the activities of some of these traders were illegal, that they were unlicensed to sell drugs in buses, but their business had thrived. There had been arrests, carried out by members of the task force on illegal drugs. But the culprits were usually set free after a few hours, because the jail was already filled with hardened criminals: kidnappers, armed robbers and murderers.

"I have in my hands," the salesman continued, "the natural key to good health. He who has health has hope, and he who has hope has everything."

There were a few murmurs from some passengers. Even the

man beside me nodded his head in approval. Someone told the salesman to speak louder, so she could hear well.

"But I believe that every human being is the author of his own health or disease," the man shouted. "A scientist may tell you that health is a state of complete physical, mental and social wellbeing, and not merely the absence of disease and infirmity. But if you ask me, I will tell you that health is the greatest gift to man."

He brought out his first product. From where I sat, I could not see the miniature bottle, but I knew what was inscribed on it: "Specially formulated dietary supplement that provides natural sources of Vitamin A and Vitamin E." I knew the words because my neighbour had been trying desperately to sell the products to me. But I was not interested in preventive or supplementary drugs. I was a fit man. I only purchased malaria drugs when the mosquitoes in my neighbourhood went berserk.

"I am in a good mood today," the salesman continued, "so I will give away these drugs for almost nothing. You are a lucky lot. I am rarely in a good mood."

"How much is it?" a passenger asked.

"For you, I will give you a bargain price of fifty naira," the man responded. "I am feeling good today. Kindly put up your hand if you want to benefit from my generosity."

A mother wanted to know if the drug could cure piles.

The salesman smiled. "I can tell you, sister. These drugs can cure anything from malaria to cholera."

I sighed. Was there a medical person in the bus? A nurse, doctor or pharmacist? Yetunde would have been livid if she had been there. I always argued that the salesmen were fresh graduates, with no jobs, who could find little else to do, but Yetunde didn't care that these salesmen were only trying to make a living. They were playing with people's lives, she said.

The cast of *The River* were already in the recording studio when I arrived at Radio Sunrise. Chief Ojo, the oldest actor, was cracking a joke about Lagos traffic wardens when I walked in. The three other actors—Tunde, Saviour and Uche—were doubled up with laughter. Trained in England, Chief Ojo had featured in a few productions in London. Sometimes he came to the studio wearing a cravat and suit trousers, garments that he claimed he brought back from Europe in the seventies.

"I have something to tell you," I announced.

"Are you increasing our wages?" Chief Ojo asked.

"I wish I could do that," I responded. I proceeded to tell them that I wanted to enter *The River* for the Radio Drama Awards in London. It had been announced that the producer of the winning drama as well as cast members would receive cash prizes and an opportunity to travel to London. Chief Ojo clapped. "Fantastic! I believe we can win. It would also be an opportunity for us to visit the BBC African Drama department."

"That's the spirit!" I said. "Let's put in our best effort today so we can win."

We began recording my script about a British man visiting Nigeria for the first time. Chief Ojo put on his British accent. Uche broke into a dirge on Nigeria. Tears welled in my eyes. The actors had brought my words to life.

I shared an office with three other reporters: Bola, Boniface and Kunle. Boniface was the oldest. He had joined the radio station when I was still in secondary school. But promotion had eluded him, so he had remained a reporter on Level 2 for more than ten years. Some people at Radio Sunrise said that the man had stepped on some very unforgiving and powerful toes. Others said that Boniface could not pass the mandatory promotion interview. But I didn't really care about the gossip. It was Boniface who taught me the rudiments of broadcasting, things I did not learn in my broadcasting module at the university: the brown envelope, for instance.

"Never cover an assignment without collecting a brown envelope," Boniface had said. "It is a real life saver for all journalists in this country."

I walked past Boniface's desk, into the gramophone library, venue of our staff meeting. Kola, the general manager of Radio Sunrise, chaired the meeting. He uttered a prayer before the meeting started.

"This is going to be a brief one," he said.

I chuckled. A brief meeting could be anything from two to four hours. Kola had been transferred recently from the Ministry of Information. He was sent to Radio Sunrise by the Special Assistant to the Minister of Information to replace the former manager who had started courting individuals who belonged to the opposition party. Kola's job description, largely unwritten, was to make sure the radio station maintained its tradition of protecting the interest of the government. He was a short man, with eyes the colour of red pepper. Behind his back, we called him Apollo Man.

"Ifiok, can you remind me what a documentary is?" Apollo Man suddenly asked.

The question hit me like a slap. All eyes in the room turned on me. I opened my mouth, closed it, and then opened it again. "Sir," I started. "Erm…"

"You have been to the training school, haven't you?" the general manager cut in.

"Yes, sir."

"Then tell me what a documentary is."

I had attended two training courses at the Radio Nigeria Training School. The first one was a course on radio production and the second was a news writing course. My writing tutor, Charles Okafor, a man of generous proportions, was a veteran broadcaster who had covered the Atlanta Olympics for Radio Nigeria. The man regularly referred to documentaries as "the aristocrats of radio."

"The purpose of documentary is to inform," I said. "It must present a story as it is, without distortion, in a balanced and truthful way, without causing offence."

The general manager clapped. "Offence! That's the word I was hoping you would mention. There is no one here who did not go to the training school. Yet yesterday, I listened to a programme that made me cringe. A programme produced by one of you. A programme that should not have been broadcast."

The rage in Apollo Man, the anger in his voice, burst out, like a great flood: "It should have been a programme to celebrate Valentine's Day. What has happened so suddenly to change the tone of good programming? What has happened?"

The man fixed his eyes on the culprit—Bola, the lady who shared my office. "You chose to describe the sexual act without any obvious inhibition! On radio!"

Bola, not used to such an avalanche of rebuke, began to sob. My poor colleague! The tears forged contours on her heavily powdered face. But the general manager would not stop his tirade. Bristling with anger, he ranted about restraint, about euphemisms and offensive words. "This is a government radio station," the man screamed. "Our salaries are paid by tax payers' money. We have a duty to broadcast quality programmes. We should not be like those private radio stations who don't know the difference between a fish and a toad!"

Bola fled to the ladies' room and Apollo Man turned to other matters on the agenda. "I am sorry to inform you that *The River* will be taken off air because the radio station can no longer afford to fund the programme," he said.

It was the way he announced the cancellation that hit me. He said it so suddenly that I almost fell off from my chair.

"Sir," I began, "I don't understand."

"Let me finish," the manager snapped.

But when he spoke further, it was obvious that the final decision had already been taken. The drama slot was replaced by a church-related programme: *Hour of Holy Anointing Fire*. The new generation of Pentecostal churches, in which the message of prosperity—that God did not like poverty—offered succour to those struggling financially in the country. They were so numerous that there were six such churches in my street. And they had enough money to buy up as much air time on radio and television as they could.

"I know the pastor behind the *Hour of Holy Anointing Fire*," Apollo Man said. "In fact, he is not just a pastor, he is an inspirational speaker. I am sure many of our listeners will be blessed by his message. I think we should consider ourselves very lucky that he chose our station to air the programme."

I stopped myself from grinding my teeth. My boss didn't care about the programme. He was not a churchgoer. Everyone in the office knew that very well. Money had exchanged hands. I had taken up producing the radio programme when the only drama producer had retired and no one else felt strongly enough about the show. It had given me great joy to use the play to take a swipe at society, something I could not do with my news reports.

In the same casual approach, Apollo Man said something

about the Minister of Information's visit to the radio station, but I wasn't listening anymore. My hearing had been dulled by the sad news of my programme's cancellation. After the meeting, I appeared at my manager's office to prevail upon him to reconsider his position. "Sir, think about my cast."

"Your cast will be fine," the manager responded glibly. "Just give them time."

I wanted to wipe that smirk off his face and tell him how ugly he was. I wanted to ask him what he would do with the money from the church programme. Would he pocket it? Would he use it to buy a gold necklace for his fat wife? But I held my peace, smiled at my boss and went back to my desk.

"How can I explain this to my cast?" I asked Boniface. "What can I tell Chief Ojo, the veteran? He is passionate about the programme, you know."

"What passion?" Boniface asked. "Why didn't his passion bring in money for the programme?"

I started. "I thought you would support..."

"I am sick and tired of that old actor!" Boniface snapped. "To tell you the truth, I am happy he will be gone. I was sick of his nosiness. I was tired of him telling us how it used to be done in England, how it must be done here. Who is he to tell us what to do? His time has passed. He is no longer relevant. I will go buy a drink to celebrate his exit. Good riddance!"

I never knew that Boniface felt so strongly about the radio drama. I had conscripted him on one occasion to play the role of a drunkard alongside Chief Ojo. He did it so well that I bought him a plate of pepper soup and beer.

I had to find a sponsor to keep the show on air.

Chapter 3

Hallelujah! Engineer Solomon had managed to deliver my car, so I was able to drive to my friend Victor's grand flat. I drove past a motley crowd of joggers along McPherson Road in Ikoyi. It wasn't a fancy car, but it made a few heads turn. I had bought it from a Chinese diplomat who was returning home after his four-year assignment in Nigeria.

I turned into the close and my car exhaust burped loudly. Some of the armed policemen stationed at Victor's block of flats leapt up. Not too long ago, the police commissioner had said that there were not enough weapons to use for fighting crime in the state. But these lot had guns that appeared to be more sophisticated than the ones held by policemen who mounted roadblocks in the streets.

One of the policeman motioned me to roll down my window. I complied.

"Who do you want to see?" he asked me.

"I want to see Victor."

"He is not in," the policeman replied. His mouth looked twisted as he glared at me.

"That is not possible," I told him. "I just spoke to him and he said he is home."

I reached for my phone and dialled Victor. When he came on line, I passed the phone to the police and he asked them to let me in. The officer with the vicious look checked my boot thoroughly before grudgingly waving me in. I noticed that as he sneered, only one side of his face moved.

Victor's apartment came with a fully-fitted kitchen with brand new appliances, master bedroom with en-suite bathroom, family bathroom and remote controlled windows. The block of flats also had a swimming pool and a gym.

"Ifiok!" Diane, Victor's girlfriend, welcomed me after I had gone through another security check at the lobby. "Come right in."

Diane was the daughter of a retired army colonel and very light-skinned. Victor had met her at a party in Abuja. Only one week later, she moved into his house, which didn't surprise me, because Victor had always liked women of fair complexion. While he was at the university, he plastered his bedroom walls with posters of such women, neatly cut from soft-sell magazines sold at Agbowo market. I followed her into the flat noticing that her dress was a bit short; I glimpsed a gleam of lavish thighs, but looked away immediately.

"Victor!"

"Ifiok!"

We embraced. My eyes were drawn to the tattoo on his left hand: a strange sign that bore a resemblance to the cross. Diane excused herself while I helped myself to some wine after checking that the percentage of alcohol was mild enough for me.

"I was reading an interesting report on Nigeria," Victor told me, nodding towards a journal he had arranged on the coffee table.

I picked up the copy of *The Economist*. On page three was a report on corrupt politicians in Nigeria. I scanned through it and saw a paragraph that said something about the government lacking the legitimacy to take harsh decisions on corruption.

"When I read such stories," Victor said, "I feel like there's no hope for this country. We're doomed."

I wanted to tell my good friend to shut his wide mouth. What did he know about doom? What did he know about hope? He worked in an oil company. His monthly salary was what I earned in a year. He lived in a good house, in a safe neighbourhood, where armed policemen stood guard twenty-four hours a day.

"You remember *The Maze*?" Victor suddenly asked. "I was thinking of our old magazine today."

The Maze was a gossip magazine that we and several other students had founded at the University of Ibadan, a student magazine that claimed to "uphold truth and defend values." Those values were interpreted as loosely as possible, because we were young and mischievous. *The Maze* reported stories of university girls who dated older men; men old enough to be their grandfathers. Some of them did it for pleasure, but many did it for the money. We got into trouble a few times, but always managed to wriggle out of it. It saddened me that I didn't have a single copy of the magazine for my library. Upon graduation, the founding editors of the publication had all gone on to pursue careers in media and communications, except Victor, who chose to work as an administrator in the oil and gas industry. Of course, his uncle played a major role in his being employed there. A few years later, Victor's position at Newman Oil put him well above all of his former classmates. That was why I approached him to get sponsorship for my drama. With a credible sponsor, I would be able to get my drama back on air.

Victor scratched his head rather loudly as I talked about the radio drama sponsorship. "I know your company can sponsor this programme. I have read on your company's website that

Newman Oil supports the arts in Nigeria, so I am counting on your sponsorship."

Victor nodded carefully. "Have you prepared a proposal?"

"Not yet," I said. "I wanted to discuss it first with you."

"Fair enough," Victor said. "Send a proposal to me when you've written it and I'll pass it on to the right person in my office who'll make a decision on it."

I thanked him. At least he hadn't laughed at me. He had listened and had promised to help. That was a good start. I thanked him again.

"Come, let's go and eat," he told me.

My stomach rumbled at the mention of food. Diane had recently graduated from a catering school in Paris. Armed with three cookbooks written by three different authors from three different continents, she churned out meal after meal after meal.

"I've made spicy seafood stew with tomatoes and lime," she announced. "Come over to the dining area, please."

Something told me it was going to be a disaster as soon as I saw the bowl of fish fillets drowned in a watery brownish sauce. I summoned up my courage to take the first spoonful. I was right. The food reminded me of rotten tomatoes and sour milk. It was torture to swallow the first bite, yet I complimented her cooking. It was what I was expected to do. I was the guest. In my village we said that you did not tell a man carrying you that he stinks.

"Very nice," I said as I played with my spoon, wondering if it would be rude to ask for ketchup to dilute the sour taste.

Diane beamed. "Thanks."

"At least all the money I invested in her catering school training was not in vain," Victor said.

It was the most torturous dinner I had ever attended. I

tried so hard to conceal my anguish that I ended up laughing too loudly at Victor's jokes. Over and over again I praised Diane's fine cookery. After the meal, I even said, "The food is so delicious. Please, could I take some away with me?"

Diane brought me bowl that was big enough to contain my head.

I let out a million farts on my way home. My poor stomach! A visit to the pharmacy in the morning was inevitable. Lagos, centre of excellence, seemed asleep as I sped along the Third Mainland Bridge. I wound down my window and flung the bowl of sour food into the river, even as a blast escaped my backside. "Good riddance to both," I muttered.

I left the window down and turned up the car radio to check for news reports on the radio. It was announced that the Ibok Youth Movement—a militant group in my hometown of Ibok—had kidnapped a foreign oil worker. I almost lost control of the steering. I thought my ears were deceiving me, but then the presenter mentioned my hometown again. I felt something cold creep down my spine. How could that be? Stories of kidnap were uncommon in that part of the Niger Delta, because Ibok people were peace-loving and friendly to visitors. It was one of the unwritten laws of the land, to treat foreigners with respect. Children even sang it:

> *Ibok people are peace loving people*
> *Ibok people are kind people*
> *They are kind to strangers*
> *They are good to strangers*

At the junction near the College of Technology, I noticed that all the motorcycle taxis that usually lined up in that area were gone. I stepped on my accelerator, not wanting to be the only one on the road. In the safety of my compound, I called my father and asked him about the kidnap.

"I knew it was going to happen," my father said. "It was only a matter of time; all the signs were there. You know old people can forecast events through simple calculations. From observations I made from other regions of the Niger Delta, I predicted that kidnapping would soon reach our community. I wrote a letter to the editor of the local newspaper to warn the government."

My father's letter occupied two columns in the paper, which he had shown to visitors in his home. "Maybe the government read it," my father continued on the phone, "maybe they did not. But at least it is on record that I warned them of this calamity."

The Ibok Youth Movement, like militants in other regions of the Niger Delta, claimed to be fighting for a more even distribution of Nigerian oil-generated wealth on behalf of the local inhabitants, who felt they were being exploited. The movement claimed that oil spills had polluted the rivers and the land, making fishing and farming impossible. They claimed that they had no means of livelihood, as they could no longer farm or fish.

My father and I debated the matter for a while. I told him, quite frankly, that some of the allegations were not true. I argued that the youths had simply copied the same message that militants used in other areas of the Niger Delta, but my father called me ignorant. When I hung up, it didn't appeal to me to sleep alone, so I drove to my girlfriend's. Since there was no traffic, I got there quickly.

"Are you worried about your parents?" Yetunde asked after she let me in to her flat.

I nodded. "I worry about my entire extended family there.

I worry too about the land itself."

Yetunde put her arms around me. "Don't worry, dear, everything will be fine. So tell me how it went with Victor."

I told her, but left out all the unfortunate details of the meal. Yetunde spread her Nigerian wax wrapper over a three-legged table and ironed while listening to me. She lifted one garment after another from a pile on the bed; she ironed them, folded them and laid each one neatly on the chair. I did not take my eyes off her. Yetunde's gestures of lifting the iron, using it, setting it down again and then folding and putting away the clothes seemed to me like an exercise in meditation.

"How much do you need this sponsorship?" Yetunde suddenly asked.

"Baby, you know that writing and producing means a lot to me. I need to get my drama back on air."

A song from a neighbour's radio floated inside the flat. Yetunde's legs began to move. It was always like that; the dialogue between her legs and music.

"You will get the sponsorship," she insisted.

"Amen," I replied.

She turned around and faced me. Her eyes seemed to say: "Believe me." And I believed her wholeheartedly. When she moved closer and her lips touched mine, I felt the familiar warmth; then the fire erupted from my stomach.

I began to fumble with my belt, but Yetunde gently told me to switch off the iron first. Once we had made love when a pot full of rice was boiling in the kitchen. It was meant to be a "short release of tension," as I called it, but it had lasted several minutes and by the time we rushed back to the kitchen, the food had turned to charcoal.

Yetunde's gown came off easily. She wore nothing underneath. Her chest grazed my back as she put her arms around me. I was afraid of turning around, afraid of spoiling the moment. But when I reached for her and held her for a while, when she fitted in my arms the way she always fitted, when I smelled her smell and felt her warmth and strength, everything fell into place.

Chapter 4

"We heard that *The River* has been taken off air," Chief Ojo said. "Is it true?"

Three executives of the National Association of Actors had come to visit me at work, unannounced. They appeared at the reception, just like that. Chief Ojo, the senior cast member of *The River*, led the delegation. It was a most unpleasant day. Our meeting room stank. Someone swore a rat must have died inside one of the drawers, so while the actors waited in reception Boniface and I spent an hour searching for it, emptying several cupboards. In the process Boniface unearthed two packs of condom: "Praise God for this find!" he said, but we couldn't find the dead rodent. Shame wanted to kill me when the actors walked in. I made up a story about water that leaked from the bathroom to the carpet and the drycleaner who was on his way to fix everything.

Chief Ojo was an old man. His heart wasn't so strong anymore. For a short while I worried that telling him the truth could make him collapse. We had no clinic in the station and the nearest hospital was some kilometres away. I did not want complications, but the man kept looking at me and I had to spit it out. "Chief Ojo, I am pleased you have come here today to talk about my radio drama," I said. "I wish I had good news for you. Unfortunately, *The River* has been taken off air."

Chief Ojo jumped up from his chair, ran to the door,

then back to his seat, threw up his hands in the air and began to wail. "So it is true! This morning, when I woke up, I was hoping you would tell me that the rumours are false. This morning, I called upon God to intervene. So it is true?"

I nodded.

"Shame on our leaders," Chief Ojo continued. "Shame on them for ignoring the arts. May our forefathers judge them!"

"So why have they taken the programme off the air?" Dele, the other actor, asked me.

"For reasons of cost," I responded.

Chief Ojo leapt up again. "Cost? How much does it cost to produce a radio drama? Ifiok, how much were you paying your actors?"

Before I could answer, he claimed that actors were not greedy people. "We act for the love of the profession," he said. "I have personally performed for free on many occasions."

"No matter how much it cost to produce the drama," Dele said, "Radio Sunrise should not have cut it. Is it not a government radio station funded by the government? Radio Sunrise is one of the few stations promoting radio drama in the country. What is going to be our fate now?"

I wished my GM would walk in then so I could point at him and say to the actors: "There is your man! The sadist who yanked the programme off the air." But my boss was in Abuja, attending a meeting convened by the wife of the Minister of Information. I had to give the actors some encouragement. It was bad for publicity to let them wander off, hot with such bad news. "I have been trying to get sponsorship for the programme," I informed the men.

Chief Ojo removed his spectacles and placed them firmly on the table. His eyelashes stood out like cat's whiskers. This man was old enough to be my grandfather, his love for the arts was remarkable; he deserved a national award. "I have been working on a proposal," I told the men. "Newman Oil has shown interest in sponsoring the programme. If that comes through, the programme will be back on air immediately."

As I told them about Victor, Chief Ojo smiled. "I am confident that you will get funding for the programme."

After the visitors left, I asked the Radio Sunrise courier to deliver the proposal to Newman Oil. Boniface thought I was being foolishly optimistic, but I didn't really blame him. Years of collecting brown envelopes had drained him of the flow of rational thought.

I left Radio Sunshine early to get ready for an outing with Yetunde. I wasn't planning to drive to the event, as I didn't know the route very well and didn't want to fall into the hands of unforgiving traffic wardens. The taxi driver arrived early to pick up me and Yetunde. The man looked like a scarecrow, and when I moved closer, I smelled alcohol. "You are drunk!" I exclaimed.

The man swore that it wasn't him. "You can go and ask my colleagues at the motor park," he said. "I don't drink much. Just a sip and I am fine. God forbid that I should be drunk."

Yetunde prayed silently before we got into the car. She called upon the Holy Spirit to keep us safe. The car, bent with age, rattled along the narrow streets crisscrossing the Yaba market. Traders sat under large umbrellas while the petrol generators beside them hummed. The streets were filled with waste—cellophane bags, banana peel, recharge cards.

We arrived on time at the wedding venue in Lawanson, a suburb of Lagos where many Efiks and Ibibios lived. The bride, Nkoyo, was Yetunde's friend. She had shocked her friends when she decided to go back to her roots to spend time in a "fattening room" specially set aside in her father's house.

Shut off from the outside world, Nkoyo spent most of the day in the room eating rice, yams, plantains, beans and gari. After many weeks of eating the food, Nkoyo was traditionally fat enough for marriage. To many of my friends, Nkoyo's size would have been alarming. I am sure my colleague Boniface would have said something about her looking like a hippo, but in the bride's culture a woman's fatness was a sign of good health and prosperity. As well as consuming a high starch diet in the fattening room, elderly people taught the bride how to be a successful wife and mother. "You must know your place as a wife," they advised. "Cook your husband good meals. When your husband is hooked on your food, he will always come home to you."

Someone shouted loudly when the bride, Nkoyo, appeared with bangles around her wrists and ankles and decorated with white chalk on her face and arms. I sat up. The well-wishers hailed the new bride, as some people broke into a song:

Behold our bride
Behold our elegant bride
She is beautiful
She is elegant

Yetunde and I clapped with the other guests as the bride danced her way to a specially built chair, covered by a canopy. She was surrounded by relatives. I knew that soon people would present the bride with gifts: pots, pans, brooms, buckets, basins, plates, glasses, table covers; everything Nkoyo would need to start her new home.

Yetunde clapped hard as Nkoyo performed ekombi, in which she twisted and twirled, shielded by maidens and resisting the advances of her husband. It was the groom's task to break through the ring and claim his bride. I was very surprised that the wedding custom still thrived. I was even more surprised that such a traditional wedding was taking place in Lagos, a city so far away from Efikland.

Yetunde suddenly grabbed my hand. "Come, let's join the dance."

"No way!" I protested.

But Yetunde dragged me to the dancing arena. I struggled to move my body, but kept bumping into people.

"I am so happy for Nkoyo," Yetunde whispered to me, as I lumbered about and she danced gracefully. "I am proud that she opted to get married the traditional way. Do you think that our marriage ceremony will be like this?"

In surprise I stepped back onto a guest's foot. Why was Yetunde talking about marriage? Had she brought me here to her friend's wedding to send me a message? I wore a tight smile and danced even more woodenly.

"Why don't you loosen up?" Yetunde asked. "Why can't you just surrender to the music?"

In the end, I did. They played "Sweet Mother", a tune that got everyone dancing like children. An old woman threw herself on the floor and cried, "This song is killing me o! This song is killing me o!"

I was a bit dizzy hours later when we left the wedding ceremony and was far from being pleased when Yetunde said we should stop by her church for a thirty-minute prayer meeting. She really wanted to pray for Nigeria, she said. After all the dancing, I wanted to go home and rest my tired legs, but Yetunde gave me that look that made it difficult for me to say no.

In the church, Yetunde quickly brought out her scarf and tied it on her head. She never prayed in public without covering her hair. The women began to sing:

Holy Spirit, come down
Holy Spirit, come down
We need you now
We need you now

I am sure Yetunde wished I would believe in the power of prayers. I am sure she wished I would allow her to sprinkle the anointing oil on my head.

"Bring your entire burden to Jesus," the pastor encouraged the congregation. "Cry out to Him. There's nothing too difficult for God. Nothing at all!"

I did not say a word. I did not join in the praying. Yetunde began to pray loudly for me. I heard her call upon God to intervene in my life.

"Pray!" the preacher commanded. "The angels are here!"

Yetunde prayed. She suddenly grabbed my hand and waved it in the air. She asked the Holy Spirit to intervene in my sponsorship. She asked the spirit to touch my heart, to make me pay more attention to God so that we can take our relationship to the next level. On our way back home, I maintained my stony silence.

Chapter 5

I left for Newman Oil immediately after I received a text message from Victor. But when I arrived, the friendly receptionist informed me that my friend was in an emergency meeting. "He said you should wait for him," she explained, as she offered me a cold drink. The Newman Oil receptionist was well-trained, unlike the rather loud receptionist at Radio Sunrise who never smiled at visitors. Her face always wore a deep frown. We often said that if you wake up in the morning and that's the first face you see, you better get back to sleep.

I did not wait long before my friend came out from his emergency meeting. Full of apologies, he ushered me to his office. He wore a smart suit and black matching shoes in contrast to the faded jeans and short-sleeved shirt I had on.

"We were in an emergency crisis meeting. There's been a community clash where we operate."

Radio Sunrise had reported that almost a hundred people were killed when a group of people from the Ibiaku community attacked residents of neighbouring Idoro community over a land dispute in the Niger Delta. "Three of our staff are missing," Victor told Ifiok. "Our oil installation in the area has been vandalised. It's not good news."

"Not at all," I agreed.

Victor said he would not be able to spend much time with me as he had another meeting shortly. His director was flying in from London and he would like to be briefed on the crisis.

"I discussed your proposal with my boss," Victor said. "He was about to make a decision today before the news of the community clash broke out."

God punish the troublemakers, I said to myself. When Victor had called me to come, I had been so sure there was good news that I had immediately bought a bottle of beer for Boniface.

"The way things are now, my boss may not be able to go back to the proposal for a while," Victor said.

"But he is still interested in the programme?" I asked.

"I would like to believe so," Victor responded. "I can't really know much, you know. I have to pretend that I don't know you."

I nodded. "I really appreciate what you are doing for me. Someday, I will thank you properly."

"What are friends for?" Victor responded as he stood up. "I have to hurry to the meeting now. Let us talk again later."

I felt hopeful as I left my friend's office and drove back to Radio Sunrise. Boniface was waiting for me at the car park.

"You have been brooding over this radio drama for some time now," he said. "This is not your father's company, you hear? You have to learn to let go. Come with me to cover an assignment. It will do you good to have a change of focus."

My colleague was a real Lagosian; his ears were always wide open. He always knew when a prominent politician was having a small party, when a new product was being launched, when an important visitor was in town. Because he had several mouths to feed, he never left an event without a brown envelope.

"I hope there won't be much traffic today," Boniface said, as we walked towards his old car.

I tried the door, but it wouldn't open. Boniface mumbled something about a dog knowing the voice of its master. The car's master detached an almost invisible bolt and the door whined and gave way. As I sat down, I prayed that the vehicle would not break down on the way.

On Radio Sunrise, playing in the car, a government official was talking about the new light rail project that would transport people within the city. "What do you think of the project?" Boniface asked.

I shrugged. "I think it is a great idea. But I hope the politicians will actually fulfil their promises. You know we have a history of abandoned projects."

"That's very true," Boniface responded.

We drove past two abandoned government buildings before we reached our destination, the New American International School, where our assignment was to report a press briefing on the school's first ten years.

The school occupied several hectares of land on Ligali Avenue that once upon a time had been a public park. Chief Richards Lanre, the current chairman of the school and a former federal minister, woke up one day and acquired the land. Just like that. People immediately protested, of course. The Ligali Avenue Residents Association organised a peaceful march to the local government headquarters. But after weeks of carrying placards, weeks of cursing Chief Lanre's penis and pouring invectives on his mother's womb, the residents of the area eventually accepted the demise of their park as the will of God. They then immediately changed their tactics to demand that their children be given priority admissions into New American International School.

"Several years ago, the idea of having an international school in Lagos would have been thought of as a foolish dream," Chief Richards Lanre declaimed. "But today, we have a private, coeducational school which offers an American educational programme for students of all nationalities in grades Pre-K through 12th."

I looked around me and noticed Simon, the reporter from *The Sun*. I also saw journalists from *The Guardian*, *The Punch* and some of the other new publications. We exchanged pleasantries.

"It is ten years today since that dream started," the chairman continued. "We are very proud of our achievements."

After the chairman's speech, the briefing continued with somebody from the principal's office showing us journalists around the school complex, pointing out the new equipment fitted in the laboratories. The tour guide, trying very hard to speak like an American, told us the high tech equipment was shipped from New York.

"We gonna make learning very interesting," he said. I tried hard not to laugh at the man's accent.

The New American International School had everything that the government schools in Lagos did not have. I gasped when we walked inside the school library which held over 20,000 books and incorporated a group instruction area, individual reference and study areas, primary age student reading room and a computer lab.

After the tour, the man handed out the brown envelopes. "It's a token from us," he explained.

It was the token that we were all waiting for. It was that token that would guarantee that the news item about the school would be published, probably that night or the next morning. My heart somersaulted when I opened the brown envelope and one hundred US dollars popped out. I had received brown envelopes in the past, but they were all meagre amounts—usually a few thousand naira. No one had ever given me dollars before, not even my uncle Phil who lived in New York. When I recovered from the shock, I turned to Boniface and thanked him for bringing me to the press briefing.

"God is great!" someone exclaimed.

"Didn't you know that before?" the reporter from *The Vanguard* said. "This morning, when I woke up, I asked Him to surprise me today!"

"Ah, this is more than a surprise," another journalist added. "I would rather call it a blessing."

I agreed that it was indeed a blessing. When Boniface dropped me off later, I walked to Island Market, to the only bureau de change that I knew. As I meandered through the market, my hands were deep in my jeans pocket, guarding the dollars that were hidden there. The traders' cries buzzed in my ears:

"I have a good bra which is the perfect size for madam."

"I only sell new second-hand chinos. You cannot find this type anywhere else in the market."

"Going! Going! Rush, while my offer lasts. No condition is permanent."

"Win your girl's heart today. Buy her my original G-string. A trial will convince you."

The traders sold everything: used boxers, handkerchiefs, briefs, socks, combs, eye pencils, bathroom slippers. When I moved towards the black market section, where the money changers were, a tall man immediately thrust his calculator at my face and asked, "I will give you the correct rate, sir. Is it pounds or dollars?"

He wore a white robe, a red cap and a wide smile. I liked him immediately. He was the sort of man who could be trusted, the sort that wouldn't want to swindle anyone. I had heard that a very large number of the money changers were cheats. One needed to be very careful.

The man's smile widened when I asked where his office was. "Just follow me," he replied. "My name is Hamza, but friends call me Don. You may call me that if you wish. I don't mind."

We walked past a man urinating in the gutter, beside him was a sign commanding: "Do not urinate here. It is prohibit."

Hamza's office served many purposes as a tailoring shop, a barber salon and a cybercafé. There was a giant poster on the wall of a happy man proclaiming: "I will laugh last." A young man eating roast plantain and groundnut shoved his food under the table as I entered the multipurpose office.

"Make room for oga," Hamza shouted at the man, "you good for nothing glutton. It is food that will kill you. How will you pass your exams when you are always eating? I do not know why I even brought you to Lagos. I should have left you in the village to continue herding cows."

When a bench was cleared for me to sit down, I noticed a yellow sticker on the side: "Relax, God is in control."

Hamza began to use another calculator, a bigger one, as he turned to me, saying. "Please, don't mind the young fool. How much do you want to change, sir?"

"One hundred dollars."

Hamza punched the calculator buttons while I watched him, still grasping my dollars firmly. Friends had advised me that I must never hand over the money until the transaction was agreed. Anything could happen to the dollars.

"That will be 14,000 naira," the man informed me.

I had, however, been tutored in the art of negotiation. I had been warned that the money changers might always want to get the best deal for themselves at my expense. "No way, Hamza. I will only agree to 16,000 naira."

The money changer laughed. "Sir, the exchange rate has dropped. If you had come last week, I would have given you what you ask for. But I can only give you 14,500 now."

We settled for 15,000 naira. He gave me the money in 200 naira notes with his business card: "Hamza Musa, Managing Director, The Don Bureau De Change. Motto: tested and trusted."

Before I took my leave, I asked him if the latest government economic policy had affected his business.

"I was born into a family of money lenders and changers," Hamza explained. "My uncle owns the largest black market in northern Nigeria. It was under his tutelage that I learnt to sniff out fake currencies from genuine originals. You see, sir, governments come, governments go, but we the money changers will be here forever."

I pocketed the money and walked to Beautiful Selections. Mr Nwachukwu smiled when he saw me. "What do you think of my kids' section, Ifiok?" he asked as he walked over to me. The man never forgot a name or a face and was always introducing new lines or arranging his old ones.

"I think it is great," I said.

"How is Yetunde?" Mr Nwachukwu asked.

"She is fine."

It was Yetunde who had made me aware that Mr. Nwachukwu had three degrees, including a MBA. "The kids' section seems to be quite popular," the trader said. "Today I have sold a few items already." He noticed my indifference, so he steered me towards the ladies' section. "You want to get something nice for your lady, eh? I will show you just what Yetunde would like."

He held up a flowered dress. "It just came in yesterday; that's why it's still here," Nwachukwu said. "If you don't decide on it now, it will surely be gone tomorrow."

I didn't like the dress, but I saw something else: denim high-waisted hot pants.

"A very good choice," the shop owner said. "I am sure that Yetunde will like them. Are you sure you don't want to add something else?"

I shook my head. "One garment is enough."

Mr Nwachukwu would not give up easily. "I can give you a good bargain. You can buy two other dresses at a reduced rate. Your girlfriend will really appreciate it. You know how our women are: the more you give them, the more love you get."

He had a sweet tongue and an open friendly face that made customers part with their money easily. I chose a floral skirt. "You won't regret it," Mr Nwachukwu said as he folded the clothes into a bag.

"Beautiful Selections" was boldly inscribed on the paper carrier bag. I had never seen it before. The last time I came with Yetunde to buy some clothes there, Mr Nwachukwu had neatly folded them into a plastic bag. "We have to protect the environment," the shop owner said seriously as he handed the bag to me. "This bag is 100 per cent recycled. It is my little contribution towards making our environment safer."

I patted the shop owner and said something about caring about the environment. It was only recently that Lagosians had started hearing of multinationals talking about cutting carbon emissions and oil companies discussing conservation and biodiversity.

"Give your girlfriend my regards," the trader told me as I left.

When I presented the gifts to Yetunde at home, she exclaimed: "Oh my God! This is so nice."

"Do you like them?" I asked.

Yetunde gave me a kiss. "I love them. Thank you very much."

We held each other for a while, then Yetunde pushed me away. "Let me try on the dress."

I watched as she slipped out of her shorts, but I couldn't resist touching her. I ran my hands along her body. "You won't let me try the dress?" she asked.

I smiled. "Not yet."

Afterwards, as we lay in each other's arms listening to Radio Sunrise, the news at dawn came on. Peter, the news reader, announced that five Chinese had been kidnapped in Ibok. This piece of information jolted me. I had thought that kidnappers only went after the Europeans and the Americans. Then the police commissioner's voice came on air, promising to flush out kidnappers from the Niger Delta. I thought the officer sounded unconvincing, like an amateur salesman. Yetunde put her arms around me and told me that everything would be fine.

Chapter 6

We stole at Radio Sunrise. Not dispossessing people of their hard-earned possessions like robbers did, but we stole news stories from other media and presented them as our own. In the beginning of my job at the station, I was horrified that journalists could do that. What had happened to ethical journalism? But Boniface had told me it was the way it worked. He had said everybody was doing it. Even international news media organisations were guilty. "Do you really believe that CNN pays for every report, from every corner of the world?" he had asked.

I was stealing stories about Abuja from *The Guardian* when the news editor instructed me to go for an emergency press conference organised by Newman Oil at the Eko Hotel. Oh, music to my ears! Perhaps my friend Victor would be there with his senior colleagues, but a big wave of disappointment hit my forehead when I arrived and didn't see him. It was the senior media officer of the oil company who had organised the press conference.

He welcomed us journalists with a very warm smile. "I am really pleased to see you all here. I am delighted that you have been able to attend this event at such short notice. I hope that your journey here will not be in vain. I hope that after today you will write more informed stories on the oil and gas industry in Nigeria."

The media officer announced that Newman Oil was shutting down production from Ibok River Field due to a surge of oil theft activities. "We are talking about people stealing tens of thousands of barrels of oil per day. My company has decided to take action in order to prevent further environmental pollution."

Oil thieves? Aha! We were a nation of thieves. I stole news stories from the CNN. The fat accountant in my station stole millions of naira with his pen. The politicians stole people's votes and declared themselves winners of elections. The rich stole from the poor. The cycle never stopped.

The media officer began to distribute some leaflets. "Illegal bunkering activities were first noticed last year," the man said, "but the government security forces moved in immediately to drive away the criminals and to destroy their stores and transport."

In the leaflets, I saw the pipelines that stretched out like felled trunks of the oil palm tree and the hacksaw cuts that had been inflicted by thieves on pipelines so that they could siphon crude oil to waiting barges and canoes.

"We have been warning the community against these acts," the media officer continued. "In fact, we hosted a seminar on the dangers of illegal bunkering and pipeline vandalism last year. Only a few people from the community attended the event. I cannot reiterate enough that apart from revenue lost to government, a large portion of the stolen oil is spilled, thereby harming the environment."

And then the media officer handed some fat brown envelopes to us. We opened them with trembling fingers, but the package only contained more leaflets, brochures and a video on oil and gas in Nigeria. There was no money.

"That press guy is an idiot," a reporter from *The Lagos Times* said. "Is it leaflets that we will eat, eh? Is it brochures that will pay my son's college fees?"

"God punish him," Linda from *Daily News* added. "He wants us to write good things about his company, yet he doesn't give us anything. Is that what they sent him to do?"

"Well, I don't know about you," another journalist said, "but for me, I will not write anything good about this oil company. All their pipelines can go up in flames, and I won't care."

I remembered comments made by a Sierra Leonean journalist about his documentary on the atrocities of his country's civil war. The journalist had said he was revealing horrors he felt nobody wanted to highlight. I reminded my colleagues about the role of journalists in uncovering social, economic and cultural developments. I pointed out that as our country's economy depended on income from oil, we should report on the illegal bunkering that was affecting our economy.

"You can go ahead and be an ethical journalist," Linda told me. "But I am not interested in that. I am only after what goes into my pocket."

To my dismay, my colleagues dumped the leaflets and walked away. Poor Newman Oil. It was clear then that the news conference would not be given coverage. For the sake of Victor, my friend at Newman, I made up my mind to write something for Radio Sunrise, perhaps for the 10am news. And so I left the room, went upstairs to the cybercafé and bought one hour's browsing time. I was in no hurry to get back to the radio station. Just as I logged on, my mother called to tell me about my uncle who had just returned from Europe with a Russian lady.

"What will he tell his wife back in Ibok?" my mother asked. "I feel sorry for the poor woman. To think that it was his wife who sold her jewellery to raise money for his air fare. Why are men like this?"

I wanted to assure my mother that I was a very different sort of man, who wouldn't betray a wife like that, but in the end I only told her that everything would be fine. After hanging up, I went through my email. My eyes lit up when I saw a note from Newman Oil. My hands were trembling as I opened the mail. The note read: "Thank you for sending us your proposal for sponsorship. After a thorough review, we are sorry to inform you that we will not be able to sponsor your programme. We hope that you will find sponsorship elsewhere."

I slumped in my chair and groaned. The lady sitting beside me in the cybercafé gave me a long look. I sat up and read the mail again. The note didn't state reasons for rejecting the sponsorship. I immediately tried to call my friend Victor, but the network was congested. After signing out and leaving the café, I called Radio Sunrise to say that my car had been involved in an accident; no injuries, but I needed to resolve the matter. I had no intention of going back to the radio station, so I went to Yetunde's place instead.

"I can't believe they turned down my offer," I told her.

Her jaw dropped. "I don't know what to say. I have prayed for God to intervene in the sponsorship proposal. Why were my prayers not answered?"

"Victor is refusing to talk to me. I have called his number several times, but I can't get through. It's not fair. It's not fair at all."

I was talking myself into a state of anxiety and I needed Yetunde to calm me down.

"Let me make you some food," she said, as she hurried into her kitchen. "A good thing I went to the market earlier to buy some yam. A nice round tuber of yam. The old lady who sold it gave me a discount. Would you like the yam fried?"

Yetunde knew that I loved fried yam, especially when it was prepared with vegetable oil.

"It won't take very long," she announced.

There was a Mexican soap opera on TV. From the costumes and the set, it was obvious the programme was quite old. Whatever had happened to the policy of supporting local content on Nigerian television stations?

"We are finished in this country," I said miserably when Yetunde came back to the living room. "Look at what we have been reduced to: watching some dated foreign programme on our national TV during prime time. My locally produced drama has been taken off air. Tell me, what hope do we have?"

"Please, don't worry," Yetunde told me. "You shouldn't worry. You will still get your programme back on air. Do not worry, please."

Yetunde sat on the edge of the chair and began to rub my head.

When Boniface heard about the Newman Oil rejection the next day, he offered to buy me a drink. "Like I always tell you," he said, "don't worry too hard. I have worked for many years in this station and I have seen many things. The most important thing is that you have a job. Concentrate on your news reporting."

"It is important for you to let go," my boss told me later, and I wondered if Boniface had told him about the rejection. "I understand your attachment to this programme," Apollo Man continued. "But let me tell you something: it was a difficult decision to take your drama programme off air. I was really hoping that you would get sponsorship for your drama so you can put it back on air and take ownership of the programme, but management had to cut it. Radio broadcasting is changing in Nigeria. There's more competition today. We need more money to run this place. We shouldn't spend money producing programmes that we are passionate about. We should spend money on programmes that listeners want. Young people in Lagos want to listen to more music. That is what we should give them."

I swallowed. The religious programmes on Radio Sunrise were all talk. Did young people want that too? But I didn't have the energy to argue with my boss. When I left the man's office, I went to see Ruth, the on-air personality who anchored a sponsored programme on shipping.

"Getting a sponsor for a radio drama will not be easy," Ruth told me. "But I can give you a name in Vision Bank to approach."

I wanted to dance Azonto. Why hadn't I spoken to Ruth earlier? Vision Bank sponsored many programmes on television and radio. They were one of the sponsors of an educational programme on CNN. I immediately called a man named Francis who was the communications consultant at the bank.

"When is the best time to see you?" I asked.

"Let me check my diary," the man responded.

There was a long pause. I tried to visualise the man on the other line. Ruth had said that he was good fellow, a true professional who would stop at nothing until a deal was sealed, but I didn't like the way she had said "deal." It had sounded like an illegal transaction.

"I think I am free on Monday next week," the man said. "Is that okay by you? Can you come to my office at 10 am?"

I smiled. "Yes, that's fine."

If the man had said Sunday night, I would have happily gone then.

"We have a deal then," Francis said.

I hung up and went to thank Ruth.

Chapter 7

News Personality of the Week was our flagship news programme at Radio Sunrise. Every week, politicians and business leaders scrambled to be featured on the show. It was understandable because guests had a full hour to sell themselves to the good people of Lagos. In principle, it was supposed to be a free platform; in reality, it came with a price. The last time we featured an aspiring senator, we had asked him to pay for the diesel in Oga's car. He understood.

I kissed my teeth when Apollo Man asked me to record an interview with the Reverend Oludare, a charismatic preacher, for *News Personality of the Week*. What a bad marketing decision! When it came to brown envelopes, the preachers were as flexible as a steel rod. To be honest, it was easier for a camel to pass through the eye of a needle than for me to be able to squeeze money from a pastor.

I had been expecting the reverend to come in a three-piece suit and his gold cross, the outfit I had seen him wear on TV, so I was taken aback by his casual dress when he walked into the studio. He wore a corduroy trousers and a white T-shirt with the caption: "For what shall it profit a man if he gains the whole world and loses his soul?" He shook my hands warmly.

"Let me set up the studio for you, then we can begin the interview," I told him. It took only a few minutes to check the sound levels of the microphones. Apollo Man had told me to concentrate on the charity work of the preacher, not his preaching.

"When we started the youth charity, the neighbours believed we would not last," the reverend said. "They said we would be out of here as soon as we began. But it's been five years and we are still here. It is the Lord's doing. I share an office with my assistant, a young man with an extraordinary gift of writing. He is the one who sends out fundraising letters to corporate organisations around the country."

"Do you normally get results?" I asked.

"Most times the organisations say that they don't fund church projects," the preacher replied. "But sometimes they do give us money. The majority of the funds are through our church members' kind donations. Without the support of brethren from the congregation, our youth project would not survive.

"When I opened the youth centre," the Reverend Oludare continued, "I faced a lot of criticism from several churches. Many bishops, reverends, pastors, whatever title they chose to bear, wrote me long, angry letters. Some even came down to my office to tell me, in raised voices, that I had no business dabbling into youth work, that I should let the government do their work.

"They wanted me to concentrate only on prayers," the Reverend Oludare said with a smile. "I remember one particular clergyman who I think had forgotten to brush his teeth that day. But I thank God for wisdom. I pointed out instances where Jesus Christ went about doing good. He didn't just pray or command things to happen. He made them happen. I told them that Jesus Christ asked us to feed his sheep."

I was surprised to learn that the reverend held a law degree from the University of London. I almost fell off my chair when he said that he had spent three years working in a top law firm in London. When he had returned to Nigeria, several firms had begged him to join them.

"I could have," the preacher admitted. "But God has called me to do something else. When I came back to Nigeria, I saw something was lacking. Our young people were being ignored. I believe the church has an important role to play in youth development. Past governments have failed us, but we cannot go on moaning: some of us have to do something. Bread of Life, our youth charity, is changing the lives of young people in this community. Just imagine if we had similar projects around the country. Think about the impact."

He told me that his charity also gave out cash awards for young people to access education, training or work. Bread of Life was also involved in conflict resolution. My mind went to the young people in my hometown fighting for survival in the creeks of the delta.

"Are you working with young people in the Niger Delta?" I asked.

The Reverend Oludare shook his head. "I would have loved to have done so, but we cannot help all the young people in Nigeria. We don't have enough funds nor the capacity to do so."

The reverend reclined on his chair, looked straight into my eyes and said, "While religious organisations like mine play a positive role in helping young people, we cannot play a larger role in the long-term development of their lives. In the end, it is left for the government to really do their work."

When we were done, I thanked the reverend and saw him to his car. For the first time in a long while, I hadn't thought about a brown envelope as the reward of my job. After the reverend had driven off, I went to report at Apollo Man's office. My boss was sprawled on his chair, eating roast plantain and groundnut. The smell of the food mixed with the smell of his carpet gave out a very unpalatable odour.

Apollo Man motioned for me to sit down. "Thank you for interviewing the reverend," my manager said. "It is our duty to tell people what good things some churches are doing in this country. Let us not always talk about the bad things that some churches are doing."

Apollo Man opened his drawer to take out a toothpick and the food and carpet smell grew stronger. Without thinking, I leaned back. Was my manager keeping some of the groundnut in there?

"I am very proud of what you are doing in Radio Sunrise," the manager said, as he picked his teeth. "We want to encourage you to keep it up. Don't mind all those other lazy reporters and producers who are just wasting government money. They don't know a change is coming. And what a change that will be!"

There had been rumours that the government was planning to retrench broadcasting funding by cutting back several jobs. A sweeping cut, they had said. Was it meant to clear out those who had refused to improve themselves? Was that the change that the manager was referring to?

"When that time comes, this place will be rid of cockroaches," the manager continued. "Only the good hands will be left. Good hands like yours. I am really sorry about your radio drama." He paused and took a long sip of water.

"I want you to act as a mentor to a new intern who has been posted to this station," my boss suddenly said. "The mentoring should take your mind off the radio drama."

I sat up, surprised. A mentor? I had never mentored anyone in my life. Such a task was better suited for someone like Boniface who had many years of broadcasting experience.

"You are a great reporter and editor," Apollo Man told me. "I love your creativity, the way you write your stories. You are a great journalist. So it makes sense for you to be a mentor."

I couldn't help smiling. Several years ago, it would have been unusual for the manager to heap such praise on his staff. It would have even been more unusual for him to say the words in front of the member of staff. Those who knew him at that time said that he preferred to commend staff through a third party. Normally, he would say to his assistant, "That was a good project. Patricia has done well." And the assistant would convey the message to Patricia.

"Don't let it go to your head, please," the manager advised me. "You must be a good mentor to this intern. Show her the ropes of broadcasting. Don't be sending her to buy you plantain and beans. You hear?"

Chapter 8

I met the intern about an hour after I left my boss' office. She was smiling as she walked over to my desk. Her face reminded me of the American singer Alicia Keys.

"You must be Mr Ifiok," she said as she extended her hands. Her voice was soft and she held my hands a little longer than was usual.

I smiled back. "And you are the new intern, Sarah. Welcome to Radio Sunrise."

She was a second year student of Mass Communications at the University of Lagos. But most importantly I learnt that she was Apollo Man's niece. It was an honour to be assigned to mentor my boss' relative. I told her she would learn a lot at Radio Sunrise.

"I hope so," Sarah said.

"I have only just got to know that you are my mentee. I will put together a routine that will work for you and make your stay here enjoyable."

"That sounds good."

In the canteen, Boniface patted my shoulder and congratulated me for having such a beauty under my care. "You lucky bastard. Make good use of the opportunity."

"What do you mean?" I feigned ignorance.

"It means that you should get down with her. Sleep with her. That's what these interns want. They are not interested in learning."

A girl in red walked past our table with a plate of beans. She was one of the other interns at the Finance Office. Her friend, who also wore red, joined her as she sat close to us. They began to eat and talk immediately.

"Can you imagine that foolish boy," the girl in red said, "that good for nothing bonga fish sent me a bunch of flowers for my birthday."

Her friend laughed and said something about dead flowers and old men. I tilted my head. My ears were aching with curiosity.

"I have told you to leave that good-for-nothing brat," her friend said. "What are you doing with a man who cannot even give you common pocket money? A man whose pockets are lined not with money, but with stones?"

"No, Agnes, in the beginning he was not a bad man."

"You are talking about the past! Did the scriptures not say that old things have passed away? Should we not move on and forget the past?"

I wondered if the ladies realised they were in a public place. They were young girls, probably in their teens. They had barely touched their food.

"I am ready to introduce you to a real man," the girl's friend was saying. "A real moneybag. He has so much money that he uses some to wipe his bottom after going to the toilet. If you are nice to him, he can send you on a trip to Europe."

"Really?"

"I know some girls that have benefited from his largesse. I know his specification. You fit it very well."

I had heard enough. I downed the last drop of my drink and then stood up. Boniface did the same.

"I told you these girls are up to no good," he said as we left the restaurant. "I call them the United Nations. They are here

53

to offer physical aid to the men in this broadcasting house. All you need to do is apply and your application will be approved. It's turn by turn. These girls are rotten."

My mobile phone rang. It was my mother who talked about what was happening in Ibok for several minutes, then my father took over. "Our land is falling right under our very eyes. And the government is doing nothing. Is it not a shame? Last week, the militants kidnapped a corpse. Yes. They went to a funeral and took away the coffin. There's no more respect for the dead. Isn't it a shame?"

I didn't know anywhere in Africa where oil brought peace, security and development. It had brought wealth for a few and misery for the rest. But I didn't say this to my mother or my father.

"Is she the daughter of a politician?" Yetunde asked later, when I told her of the new intern.

"She is my boss' niece," I responded.

I had hoped that telling Yetunde about the girl would make me stop thinking about her. I had found it hard to forget her smile, her dimples and the goodbye hug she gave me in the recording studio.

"You will be careful, won't you?" Yetunde asked.

I nodded, although I didn't understand what she meant. Yetunde got up and I watched her. For the first time since we had been dating, I compared her with another woman, a younger woman for that matter. It shamed me. She turned around so I could unzip her. As I did so, I let my hands run along her bare back. She gently pushed me away and went to the kitchen to prepare pounded yam and efo soup. I hovered around the tiny kitchen as Yetunde chopped the leaves into thin slices. It was one thing I could never do well despite several years of tutelage in my mother's kitchen.

"Where is the yam flour?" I asked.

Yetunde pointed to the cupboard that housed the yam flour. Sometimes she complained that the packaged flour contained too much preservative, that it tasted nothing like the yams that went through the natural process of cooking and pounding.

"I hope there's enough gas in the cylinder," I said, as she stirred the pounded yam vigorously.

"There had better be o," Yetunde replied. "It had better last us till we finish cooking this meal."

We. I liked the way she used the plural term. Though my contribution to the cooking was negligible, I felt pleased that it was significant to her. When the food was ready, we ate off the plastic serving dish that she had brought back from yet another wedding. A picture of the bride decorated it with the inscription: "Yemi weds Robert. Courtesy of the Afolabi family."

Chapter 9

"Hot spots" were what we in the news room called the several places in Lagos Island that we dared not drive our cars to. Martin Street was a hot spot, a nest of petty crimes and criminals. On Martin Street, people's bags were snatched in broad daylight while pedestrians walked past as if nothing happened. I had been accosted there once by a tall guy whose teeth were the colour of ripe mango. What frightened me most about the encounter was the calmness in which he had spoken and the impeccable English that had flowed from his mouth: "I am really sorry for disturbing you, sir. But I need to dispossess you of your wallet and wrist watch." It was in the middle of this madness that Vision Bank had their headquarters.

I wore the only suit I owned to meet Francis, the communications consultant at the bank. I arrived several minutes early and was asked to wait at reception.

"Francis will see you now," the receptionist told me, almost an hour later. "Have you been here before?"

"No," I responded.

She gave me a visitor's tag. "Down the corridor. Turn left. It's the last door."

It sounded easy to locate. But when I walked down the corridor, it was difficult to tell which door was the last. I turned the door knob and walked into the men's toilet. I ran out immediately and wondered why the door wasn't labelled.

The next door I tried led to a kitchen. Francis' office was behind the third door.

"Nice to meet you, Ifiok," Francis welcomed me.

"Nice to meet you too," I said, immediately falling in love with his blue suit.

Francis didn't have a large office. There was only space for two chairs as most of the office was taken over by cabinets. "Shall we get straight to business?" he asked.

I felt rushed. I would have preferred to find out a bit more about Francis and his qualifications. Was he a communications graduate? But the man obviously was not interested in pleasantries.

"What is the proposal about?" he asked me.

I cleared my throat and gave him a quick outline of my radio drama. "I have already prepared a proposal for sponsorship," I said, handing over the document.

Francis collected it and dropped it on his desk without a glance. "I am going to be straight with you," he said. "Vision Bank gets a lot of proposals for sponsorship. Some of them are pretty good ideas. Unfortunately, we cannot sponsor them all."

"I understand," I said.

"Good," Francis said. "Most proposals come straight to me. I do the preliminary analysis. I read the proposal and decide if my bosses should see it or not. Ultimately, the top guys make a final decision, but I am the man at the door. If I think a proposal is silly, the top guys won't even get to see it. I send it straight to the bin. Do you get me?"

Francis was indeed an important man. I owed Ruth more than a thank you. I intended to get her something particularly nice from a boutique.

"Because I spend so much time reading these proposals, I

often ask for a little token," Francis said. "It's not compulsory, of course, but it makes sense for someone who has taken the time to write a proposal to make sure that his letter will be attended to."

I understood exactly what Francis was saying, but I had never imagined that bankers would ask for a gratification. They weren't poorly paid like us journalists. They wore smart suits and were sweet talkers. "You don't have to give me anything now," Francis said. "Go home and think about it. When you are ready, you can come back."

"How much are we talking about here?" I asked.

Francis glanced at the proposal. "Since this is a radio project, I would say about 100,000 naira."

100,000! That was worth two months of my own salary. Francis noticed my shock. He coughed and said, "As I said, go and think about it. Come back when you are ready."

I picked up my proposal. "Yes." I nodded as calmly as I could. "I will think about it."

As I meandered on my way out of Martin Street, I knew the end had come. Everyone had been right. The radio drama had been killed. Rest in peace, *The River*! I sent a text to the cast of the play. The actors began to call me back immediately, but I was not man enough to pick their calls.

"A big fat shame," Chief Ojo, the veteran, texted back. "The only drama on radio has been discontinued. What do we tell our children?"

"I am happy that you have decided to let it go," Yetunde said later, when she came over to my flat.

As we lay down together, my mind went back to when we first met. Before Yetunde met me, her life had been turned upside down by the untimely death of her father. Yetunde kept the obituary of her father, the one that had appeared in the local newspaper, tucked away in her trunk box. On some nights, she brought it out and spread it on the bed. Sam, her late father's distant relative who worked as a technician at the media house, was able to place the notice for free. For that, Yetunde's family had been very grateful.

Yetunde's father had made lots of sacrifices for her. He had worked as a driver, and though his salary had been poor, he had sent Yetunde to school. His friends and colleagues had asked him, "Why are you wasting time and money training a woman?" But the man had always replied that education should be a right and not a privilege. He had been Yetunde's mentor. He had taught her to believe in herself and the works of her hands.

Yetunde had mourned her father for a long while until I came along and wiped her tears away. We had met at the hospital where I had gone to interview a patient. A young boy, running from a nurse's injection, had knocked over Yetunde's tray. I had immediately told her not to worry and had got up from my chair, knelt down to pick up the contents of the tray. She told me later that at that moment, my voice had sounded like her father's.

Chapter 10

I took Sarah, the intern, through a crash course on the history of our work at the radio station. I told her about the various directors and their different visions for Radio Sunrise, like Alhaji Usman, a former Director General, who had introduced news reading in the Hausa language. I told her about the year the radio station could not broadcast any programme because the transmitter was stolen. I told her about the bitter union strike, when we were at home for three months. I told her about the day soldiers stormed the station to take away a presenter who had been playing martial music on air. I told her how Radio Sunrise faked winners of a game show. Sarah was a good listener. I knew she was interested because she smiled or frowned in just the right places.

I took the intern on her first assignment: a press conference organised by the Nigerian Police. They never gave brown envelopes, these policemen, but I always attended their press conference to keep a positive relationship with the Police Force Public Relations Office. A good reporter needed to know a police officer to turn to, especially in an era of indiscriminate arrests and detention.

When Sarah and I arrived at the press conference, some reporters were already there. I walked up to Emeka, the crime reporter from *The Daily Sun*. We had covered events together in the past.

"So you are here?" I asked.

"If I am not here, who will be?" Emeka responded.

We gathered in small groups as we discussed what news the police would be announcing. We decided to do some guessing, trading a few suggestions. Some of the reporters swore the press conference had to do with the rise of traffic offences in Lagos. Some said it had to do with the upcoming Lagos Carnival.

"I can confirm that it's about the Lagos Carnival," Emeka said. "The Brazilians arrived last night and we are expecting more people from around the world. I am sure the police will tell us what plans they have regarding security."

The Police Public Relations Officer came out to address us journalists and gasps filled the room when he announced that his men were holding a goat on suspicion of attempted armed robbery in addition to claims that it used juju to change from a human being to escape justice. "Vigilantes brought the animal to us, claiming it had been a person trying to steal a car," the policeman said.

The pen fell from my hand. I knew that the police could arrest anyone they wanted, but I didn't know their jurisdiction included animals! I picked up my pen and adjusted my voice recorder. Another bizarre story to add to my growing collection.

The policeman continued, "The group of vigilante men came to report that while they were on patrol they saw some hoodlums attempting to rob a car. They pursued them. However, one of them escaped while the other turned into a goat. We cannot confirm the story, but the goat is in our custody. Let me assure you that we cannot base our investigation on something mystical. It is something that has to be proved scientifically."

When we recovered from the shock, the questions flew out from our mouths: Could we see the goat? Was it a male or female goat? Was it a Nigerian goat? How big was the goat? And the police officer answered as many questions as he could, and then he went to fetch the thieving goat.

"I bet you didn't know we covered such bizarre stories," I said to Sarah later when we left the police station.

"It's unbelievable," the girl responded.

She said she was hungry and I dropped her off at an eatery near my house. I gave her some money and bid her goodbye. At home, I switched on my laptop and tried to edit some of the materials from the press conference. I had recently installed an editing software on my laptop, but as soon as the stress of the day let go of me, I succumbed to sleep.

A knock roused me later.

"Who is there?" I asked.

Yetunde had said that I should always ask because the fear of thieves is the beginning of wisdom. "It is me, Sarah."

Sarah! What did she want? I opened the door. The girl was still wearing her blue jeans and she had a plastic bag in her right hand. "Good day," she said.

I did not answer the greeting. "How did you find out where I live?"

The girl stood back and smiled at me. The smile deflated me, confused me so that I stepped aside quickly. "I asked around for your address," the girl said. "Don't you know you are famous? A lot of people know where you live." Was I famous? I didn't know whether it was a good or bad thing.

"I brought you some food from the eatery," Sarah said and then placed the bag on the centre table. She moved about the room, her hands touching everything: the three-legged table, my graduation picture on the wall, the grandfather clock.

"Won't you open it?" she asked.

I looked at the bag. "What food is inside?"

Sarah's eyes sparkled. "Why not open it?"

I did not really want to open the bag, but the girl's eyes begged me to do so. When I finally did, the aroma of fried rice hit my nose, forcing me to catch my breath. Sarah was staring at me. Her eyes suddenly frightened me. My neck throbbed. I felt the familiar fever, the stirring in my loins. I remembered Boniface's words about interns and free sex.

"Should I feed you?" Sarah asked.

"Pardon?"

She laughed. "Do you think I'm a little girl?"

"I didn't say that." I told myself that I was playing with fire. "Does your uncle, my boss know you are here?"

She looked away. "I just brought you food. I know you are a bachelor. You probably have not eaten all day. It was only fair for me to bring you food."

"Thank you."

She swung her young bosom around the sitting room. I could not stop my eyes from following her movements. The girl's eyes rested on the films on my desk.

"Do you watch a lot of Nigerian movies?"

"Sometimes. But these days I rarely have the time to watch any film at all."

"You should watch *Emotional Crack*," she cried. "It is a fantastic story about a young woman who is a lesbian. I loved that film!"

"Really?"

"Oh, yes!"

I swallowed. "You should go now."

"Sir, please…"

"Please go."

She frowned. I took two steps towards her. I patted her shoulders, and a smile warmed her face. "You are a handsome man, Ifiok."

"You really should go now," I said as I pushed her away.

"Please, let me stay for a while," the girl begged.

"It's not a good idea," I responded. "What if your uncle looks for you?"

The girl surrendered. "Okay, I will go. Please eat your food before it gets cold."

I exhaled a deep breath when she was gone. I sat on the sofa and watched the food that I would not eat. The world was an unsafe place. I had heard bizarre stories of young girls who trapped men with their love-potioned delicacies. I looked at the food again and decided that although I would pour it away, I would not tell Yetunde about the visit. But I did tell Boniface the next day and he let out a long whistle, which made a few people in the canteen look over at us.

"You mean she was at your place? I bet she was good, eh? Tell me everything. I want to hear the details."

"There's nothing to tell."

"Meaning?"

"Nothing happened. Simple."

"You are joking. A young girl walks into your house and offers herself to you, but you threw her out. Are you normal?"

I dropped my spoon in the plate. Someone in the restaurant started to sing out loud. It was a song about God's goodness.

"Have you won the jackpot?" a customer asked the singer.

"Tell us, please," another added, "so we can join you in praising God."

Boniface turned to me. "Are you really saying nothing happened?"

"I swear nothing happened."

Boniface got up and left the canteen. At the door, he almost bumped into a scar-faced man from the Ministry of Water Resources, next door to Radio Sunrise. I had seen the man a couple of times. He had the look of a vagrant. Sometimes, he came into the restaurant dressed in his frayed coat; at other times, he wore a Russian hat.

I noticed that Scar-face looked very serious as he sat and waited for his order. There was an empty bottle of drink on his table. When the waiter bent down to clear away the bottle, Scar-face began to curse. "You silly Ibo man! You are just the type that shouldn't be in this city. I wish you were dead. I cannot…" His rant seemed endless. I liked that waiter. He had a face that made you feel sorry for him. Scar-face talked into a feverish state, his eyes bleary. Was it the chair that had triggered something in him? Was it the air? Scar-face continued cursing all non-Yorubas. When he began swearing at the president, the manager hurried in and asked him to leave.

"I'm not leaving!" the man screamed. "It is this fellow who should leave. He shouldn't be here."

"You should be ashamed of yourself," the manager said.

"For telling the truth? This is my city, mate. This is my land!"

This is my land! It sounded strange to my ears. Which land did he mean? His words worried me, reminding me that there were lots of crazy people in Lagos. The uncouth man would not stop talking. "Nigeria is a country of several states. Everyone should go back to his or her state. People who are not from Lagos should leave. Lagos is full. No more space for foreigners. I have had enough."

People too had had enough of the man. Enough of his face. Enough of the smell of his coat. They asked him to carry his evil mouth and legs out of the canteen.

"It is people like you," someone shouted, "that want to spoil the peace of this city. What is your problem, eh? Did they send you? Did the crisis mongers send you?"

"Perhaps he has sniffed something today," another customer called out. "If I tell you what a lot of people sniff these days, you will collapse. Yesterday, I saw my neighbour sniffing lizard shit."

"Lizard shit?" another customer asked.

"You heard me," the other customer replied. "Lizard shit. It stands to reason that someone's mind would be messed up when he sniffs shit?"

A man beside me asked, "What's all this nonsense about shit? Have you forgotten that I am eating?"

I shook my head. When the scar-faced man stood up and staggered out, I wondered if he would return the next day.

Yetunde was at work later that day, and I was trying to prepare fish stew for myself when Sarah appeared again at my flat. She wore a flimsy blouse that advertised her cleavage. I had seen a blouse like that worn by a dancer in Davido's videos. She said she had come to borrow some films from me. I was reluctant to let her inside the flat so I held on to the door frame, when she strode inside my kitchen and opened the pot. "Someone is cooking!" Sarah said. My fear of love potions returned.

"Do you have everything here?" Sarah asked. "Chicken, pepper, salt, onions?"

Sarah quickly figured out where everything was, finding the ground pepper in the old Ovaltine can. I gave up and closed the door.

"The electricity people have been kind to you this evening," Sarah said. "This same time last night, was there power?"

I wished the girl would stop talking, but she did not care.

She talked about the latest film, about which actor was dating which other celebrity, about a Nigerian footballer in Arsenal, about the English premier league. "You know I am an Arsenal fan," she announced.

The food scalded my tongue when I tasted it. She had added too much pepper. "Do you want to kill me?" I exclaimed.

She laughed. "Haba, Ifiok. Pepper is good for the body."

I had to admit that despite the fieriness of pepper, the food tasted really good. I noticed, as we talked on, that she didn't say anything about the film she came to collect. Perhaps it was the girl's blouse. Perhaps it was the way she skipped across the room. Or maybe there was something in the food that triggered the lust. She touched me first. When I fumbled with her trousers, she wriggled out of them quickly. She wore nothing underneath her clothes. I didn't even carry her into the bedroom. Everything happened right there in the living room.

When it was over, she pulled me into her arms and stroked my head. With my ear against her chest, I could hear the pulse of her blood, the steady thump of her heart, and they seemed to slow as I listened. Someone in an upstairs flat shouted out, but when I attempted to get up, the girl drew me back to the sofa.

"Stay with me," she whispered. "Hold me. I have always been attracted to older guys. Though I have a boyfriend who is my age mate, I find him too silly, too young to understand the act of lovemaking." She chattered about her private life, the first time she made love, the forty-year-old man who deflowered her in the back of his Nissan car. He was her friend's daddy, she said with a giggle. There had been many other older men: her class teacher, the neighbour, Mike who had three children.

"I love sex," she said. "I cannot seem to get enough of it. I have cheated on my boyfriend so many times that I have lost count. I cannot help it."

She leaned back and started to kiss me, but I pushed her away. When she eventually left, her smell lingered in the room. I shuddered. The odour in the room got thicker and more oppressive. My nostrils twitched as the smell flowed into me, past me. It clawed at my throat. Nausea overwhelmed me. I rushed to the toilet.

My palms were sweating when I called Yetunde. "I just wanted to tell you that I love you," I said.

"That's so sweet," she replied. "Is everything okay?"

"Everything is fine. Can't I just call my woman and tell her I love her?"

"You haven't done that in a while," Yetunde responded. "So what's up?"

My palms were sweating profusely. "I was just missing you."

"That's so sweet," she said again. "Now, I have to get back to work. I will see you tomorrow."

I sat on my sofa and stared for many minutes at the space Sarah had occupied. Then I sighed.

Chapter 11

I drove to the hospital the next day to pick up Yetunde from work. I had ironed my best traditional outfit with spray starch. I even wore a matching hat. My gateman struggled to recognise me. His mouth was still wide open even after I had driven the car out of the compound. "Please, make sure you close the gate and your mouth!" I called out to him.

Yetunde's hospital was at the end of Lara Lane, a road so riddled with potholes it was impossible to drive straight down it. My car lurched this and that way, like a break-dancer. At some point it spun into a bit of gyration. I gripped the steering as I was forced to join in the evil groove. I thought of the number of patients who danced their way to death.

Because Yetunde had not quite finished her shift, I waited for her at a nearby food kiosk that was popular among workers around the hospital. As soon as Mama Bayo, the lady who sold fried yam at the kiosk saw me, she wiped a wooden stool for me to sit down. Then she started talking, telling me everything that happened to her that day, like the patient who had snuck out of the hospital because he had no money to settle his bill.

"He must have planned it with the security guard," she said, "because there was no one at the gate when he got there. He walked right out of the gate. If not for the male nurse who was here buying yam, he would have walked away free."

Mama Bayo apologised for the smoke that wafted towards

me. She swore by her right arm that she would soon buy a portable gas cooker. She assured me that the next time I visited I would see a new kiosk, fully branded. I didn't doubt the new stall. After all, the telecom companies were busy giving out branded kiosks. It was the cooker I was worried about. People bought her yam because it was prepared with firewood. People savoured the smoke that came with the food, the type of smoke they wouldn't get from gas.

"It is not very cold," the woman said when she produced my drink. "I hope you can manage with it like that. The electricity in this area has been fluctuating. You don't work around this area, do you? I don't remember seeing you here. And I never forget a customer's face."

I smiled. "No, I don't work around this place. I work on the other side of the city, on the island. I came here to meet someone."

"You must be working in the banks," the woman said. "One of those new banks in Victoria Island. Abi?"

I shook my head. "As a matter of fact I do not. I am a radio broadcaster."

The woman smiled. "Then you must go and report on your radio station how foreign fast food restaurants have killed my trade. People used to be very happy eating my fried yam and akara, now they want to go to KFC."

"Are you serious?" I asked.

"Believe me. Even houseboys and housegirls steal their masters' money just to have a taste of foreign fast food."

When I laughed, the woman reprimanded me, "It is not a laughing matter."

Stupid me. I shouldn't have laughed. The poor woman was probably married to some vagabond man who lived in a Godforsaken part of town with three other wives and many more concubines, women who sapped him of his energy and whatever earnings he made. Mama Bayo most likely had seven ravenous mouths to feed every day, and had to look after them all by herself, from her meagre earnings. No, I shouldn't have laughed.

Yetunde arrived a while later and Mama Bayo embraced me. "You didn't tell me you were Yetunde's husband," she berated me. "She's my best customer."

I smiled. "Now you know."

Yetunde put her arm around me and we walked towards my car. I endured another tortured drive on the damned road but we made it unscathed to the Indian restaurant in Awolowo Road, three blocks away from a popular Chinese take-away. I found parking behind an abandoned Portacabin. While my girlfriend waited in the car, I answered the call of nature and tried not to watch my piss water the lawn. I finished my business, turned around and came face to face with Boniface! I rubbed my eyes wishing they were playing tricks on me. How did he know we would be there?

"I saw you crossing the road as I was driving past," he said, as if reading my mind. "Now that I have seen you, you cannot go in without me. God will not allow it."

"Boniface, you are not invited," I cried. "Not today, at least. I am with my woman."

"So?" Boniface asked. "Are we not colleagues? Do we not share the same office? I have been there for you, Ifiok, all the way. I encouraged you, when you felt let down. Ifiok, look me in the eye and tell me to go away."

I couldn't. Yetunde came out of the car and we all trudged into the restaurant. Fela's music filled the air. It was a song about the dilemma of Nigerians, about suffering and smiling. Boniface broke into a dance. "Fela is playing in an Indian restaurant," he cried. "God be praised!" I pulled him to the next available seat.

The waiter took our order of chicken tikka masala. He took an extra minute to explain that the meal of boneless chicken tikka was mildly spiced and delicately prepared in special masala sauce. I salivated. Yetunde said she wanted her food very spicy.

"Me too," Boniface said.

"Are you sure that your stomach can tolerate this food, Boniface?" I teased. "I am sure all your life you have only eaten local dishes. I don't want the Indian food to cause wahala inside your body. I don't have the energy to rush you to the hospital."

"We will see, won't we?" Boniface responded.

He poured praise on the pretty lady who brought the order. She had wheeled the assorted food to us on a white trolley. "This is what I call service," he said.

I did not know if my colleague was referring to the food, the polished tables or the air-conditioned room. Perhaps he was even alluding to the lady's body. When she bent to adjust our plates, Boniface had a good view of her cleavage, and I was sure his dirty mind had ripped off the waitress' immaculate uniform, to visualise what lay beneath. I tried not to think of such foolish things.

"Who would have thought ten years ago that middle-class Nigerians would be eating so comfortably at an Indian restaurant?" I asked.

Yetunde arranged her fork. "It is the dividend of democracy. I still remember clearly when we had only one proper eatery on the entire Lagos mainland. Just one eatery."

We ate slowly. It was not the sort of place where you hurried over a meal. Around us were men and women in fashionable clothes. I was happy with what I was wearing, but Boniface was the odd man out with his flowered short-sleeved shirt, the sort of thing my dad would have worn to the farm.

"I once worked as a waiter," Boniface suddenly said.

I looked up from my plate. "When? Where?"

"In England."

I grunted. I could have sworn that the man had never left the Lagos Murtala Mohammed International Airport. "I will swear on this plate of food that you have never left Lagos," I declared. "So stop lying."

Boniface laughed, then said, "In England, my hands held many cleaning liquids, many napkins. I perfected the art of polishing tables, chairs and the cold floor. My manager, Suzie, believed I was the right man for the job and she wrote nice reports about me to the head office in London. I still remember those reports."

"Why don't you tell us how you got to England?" I asked. "Did you go by road or ship? I want to know."

Boniface looked up from his food. "When I was given an award from the head office, Suzie was elated. I still remember the glossy certificate and the chairman's imposing signature. That same day, I met an old African man. He had spent twenty-five years cleaning floors. Poverty was written all over his face. It was then I realised I could never make it in England. I tore up my award and thrust it in the bin. Then I packed my bags and came back to Nigeria."

"Good thing you came back," I said. "Otherwise you would have been deported by the authorities."

Yetunde suddenly coughed, a dry cough that caught the attention of a waiter. "Is everything okay?" he asked.

"Yes, I am fine," Yetunde said.

I was not fine. My deep regret was Boniface's presence.

I had hoped to be alone with Yetunde, so I could say sweet things to her, like that she was the only sugar in my tea, the bone of my bone. I wanted to declare my undying love for her and wash the terrible guilt of infidelity away.

Chapter 12

"The Chinese are here! The Chinese are here!" the street urchins sang.

I was at the phone shop down the road from Radio Sunrise. Chuks, the shop owner, was trying to unlock the mobile phone I had recently bought in Ikeja.

"The Chinese are here!" the kids cried out again. I ran outside. Indeed, crawling up the street was a truck made by a Chinese company; a Chinese-manufactured bulldozer following close behind. In Lagos, the Chinese were everywhere, but people loved them. We loved the cheap electronics they made available at the shops in Ikeja and Alaba. We loved the expressways and the railways they were constructing in the city.

The men who jumped out of the truck were not Chinese and they hadn't come to fix the roads or sell cheap phones. They were members of the government clean-up agency. The officials, twenty of them in total, sang and marched straight to a food kiosk which wasn't really a threat to The Lord is My Shepherd Foods. I had eaten there only once. Perhaps I had chosen the wrong soup or the wrong time or the wrong day, but their food had tasted so bad that I never went there again.

I took out my recorder. I was at the right scene at the right time. The government officials formed a circle around the canteen which was made of corrugated roofing panels. The chief cook appeared at the door. She was a very imposing woman. I had heard that her husband, a man who hailed from the western part of the country, had fled when he found it increasingly more difficult to satisfy her sexual urges.

The chief cook grabbed one of the government officials and lifted him off the ground.

"You think you can come here and destroy our business?" she screamed. "I will let you know that this is my territory. I will teach you the lesson of your life."

"Put me down immediately!" the official demanded, his feet waving in the air like a tattered flag. "You are operating an illegal canteen. We must destroy it!"

His colleagues, worried for the man's safety, hit the woman with pans, pots, batons, anything that came their way. One of the officials slipped and fell into a bucket of palm oil.

"I am finished!" the cook wailed after her hold on the man had been loosened. "I am finished!"

The bulldozer crept towards the canteen. I recorded every sound, including the voices of the customers who joined in the plea to save the eatery from demolition. No amount of begging seemed able to halt the vehicle's advancement. The bulldozer nudged the kiosk and the roof clattered down.

"If only they had let me finish my lunch," a customer lamented. "I had waited twenty minutes to be served. Do they not know that a hungry man is an angry man?"

The officials moved towards Musa's cubicle which was next to the bulldozed canteen. The man immediately fished out his dagger. This kind northerner had been a good friend of the local community. Most people in the street, me included, relished Musa's tasty suya.

"Kai, you will not come near me," Musa threatened the

officials. "You will not destroy my business. God will not allow it."

But Musa was powerless against twenty strong men of the government. His stall was given the same treatment as the eatery.

"Ah, no one warned me that Lagos would be like this," Hauwa, his youngest wife, cried. "I wouldn't have come o!"

Interestingly, the Lord Is My Shepherd Foods' building was spared. I approached the leader of the government delegation for an interview. He told me the government was determined to rid the city of unapproved buildings. He spoke about the regeneration efforts of the government, how they were knocking down the old prison and converting it into a park. It became material for my city news.

When I got back to the station, Sarah gave me a smile that made my throat dry. Her voice sounded very excited, as she greeted me, "Good afternoon, Ifiok. I hope your day has gone well." In the studio, when we were alone, I told the girl that our relationship should remain very professional.

Sarah smiled. "I dreamt of you last night."

Anger swam inside me. "Don't you get it? I have behaved very irresponsibly. I won't do that again. Today, I want us to go and cover an assignment on Nollywood."

The manager had asked me to do a story on the Nigerian film sector for the weekend show because Femi, the entertainment producer, was in the hospital. In the radio station, people called Femi "Mr Nollywood" since he knew the movie sector like the back of his hand. He had a sticker on his car that read: "Nollywood is one of Nigeria's positive cultural contributions to the international community. Support it." He could interview anyone he wanted, he always boasted, be it Genevieve Nnaji or Monalisa Chinda.

Sarah jumped into my car and, as I drove off, she started painting her face. I tried to look ahead, ignoring the whiffs of powder that wafted my way. I kept a straight face as she ransacked my car in search of music CDs.

"Don't you have Tuface in your car?" she asked, but I gave no response.

The National Theatre was an architectural masterpiece, a cultural landmark and a melting pot of actors, musicians and other artistes. The building always reminded me of a sailor's cap. It was said that the design was taken from the Palace of Culture and Sports in Varna, Bulgaria.

When we arrived, some artistes were arguing about football. I cleared my throat and introduced myself, Sarah and the purpose of our visit.

"Haven't you come in a bit late?" Dino, an actor, asked. I had seen his face in a few Nollywood movies.

"I don't understand," I responded.

"Why would you understand?" the actor asked. "You Lagos journalists don't understand anything. You go about with your archaic recording equipment to conduct interviews…"

"What interviews?" another actor cut in. "You call those spiteful things they publish interviews?"

"They are blinded by money, these journalists," Dino said. "For your information, we don't have a brown envelope to give you."

Perhaps Mr Nollywood had a technique for dealing with these actors, but I didn't know if the artistes were putting on a performance just for me, so I held my peace. I was there for an official assignment. "Sir, you do not need to give me any brown envelope," I said.

"But you are late!" Dino said. "Last week, the BBC was here to interview us. Where were you?"

"Point of correction," Moses, the other actor said. "They were here to interview some of us."

Dino grunted. "It doesn't matter if they interviewed me or you or only a few of us. The important thing is that they interviewed us about our industry: Nollywood. They came all the way from London. And boy, what an interview!"

Moses nodded. "Yes, we told them everything: how we started; how we have grown; how the government has refused to support us."

"Oh yes," a good-looking actor added, "no external funding from the government or corporate organisations. The journalist could not believe his ears."

"It was an extensive and intelligent interview, mind you," Dino said. "How I wish it had been a Nigerian journalist. But…"

"I am sure we can do better," Sarah spoke for the first time and smiled her sweet smile. The actors looked at her.

Dino shook his head and for a moment his lips moved but no words came out. "Better late than never," the man said finally. "So what do you want to ask?"

I asked them about the alleged banning of artistes. I had heard that some movie marketers were refusing to sell movies that featured certain actors. This was a first in Nigeria.

"It is a shame that an illiterate marketer would choose to dictate to us," Dino said. "If I say my fee is one million naira, why should I be banned because of that? I am not forcing anyone to pay me that."

"So the dispute is about fees then," I said.

"Yes, it is about money," Moses said. "They want to destroy our industry. God will not allow it. Our industry will not be destroyed!"

I recorded the actors' rant, along with their rebukes and

praises. The interview over, Dino offered to take me along to his set where he was recording a movie entitled *Diary of Sweet Sugar Mummy*. The shoot took place in a well-furnished living room. In Lagos, a man was judged by how good his living room looked. A rich man's living room had glass tables, flat-screen TVs, home theatre, Persian rugs and leather chairs.

"The owner of this house lives in America," the director of the production told me. "His brother arranged for us to use it." Lowering his head, he added, "I hope the owner doesn't find out."

It was late in the afternoon and some of the actors were looking dazed. Someone explained to me that it was because they had been working for seven hours without interruption. I thought of the long breaks I used to give the cast of my radio play and the fried yam and soft drinks I bought for them from my own pocket.

Just when the Nollywood crew was about to conclude the day's shoot, the diesel generator, their only source of power, broke down so they couldn't continue.

The producer turned to me. "Don't worry, my brother. These things happen. Nollywood will get there. Believe me, we will get to that promised land."

If only Sarah had gone straight home after the interviews. If only she hadn't followed me back to the office to collect her stuff, as she had said. Maybe it was the smell of the studio. Maybe it was the equipment. When our eyes met, when our hands touched, nothing else mattered. The recording studio equipment was the silent witness to our lovemaking.

I zipped up my trousers with shaking hands. What man did it with an intern in a recording studio? Her uncle could have caught us. Her juices could have dripped on the table and the studio manager, a devout Christian, could have made trouble. He would have called on the God of Abraham to fry my arse. I had heard him say such prayers in the studio. Fire prayer, we called it.

I ran into Boniface in the corridor and he swore he could smell the sex on my shirt. I squirmed. I sought his help in resisting the advances of Sarah, but my colleague laughed.

"You must be kidding," he said. "What sort of a man are you?"

"For goodness sake, Boniface. I have a girlfriend. Sarah is an intern. I should be mentoring her, looking after her."

"But that's what you are doing," Boniface said calmly. "You are mentoring her body, which is a very good thing."

And despite my swearing and my guilt, despite telling myself that I was ready to cut off the "offending thing" between my legs, I could not say no when Sarah followed me home that evening. In my living room, she put the CD on and Tuface's music filled the air.

"Dance with me," Sarah said as she pulled me to my feet.

I yielded. It was easy to dance with Sarah. I liked the way she encouraged me with her eyes and smile, the way her soft hands held my fingers. Sarah danced out of her clothes. She made me fall in love all over again with Tuface. Suddenly, the musician was speaking to me, to my soul. Suddenly, I felt myself being lifted. Higher, higher, higher.

"You are not doing badly as a dancer," Sarah whispered in my ears.

When Yetunde walked in on us, we were both naked and dancing in each other's arms.

Chapter 13

I shut the door, stepped out into the road and thrust my hands in my pockets.

Had my desire to "release some tension" not been so dire, I would have remembered to lock the door. It was her silence that shocked me, the way Yetunde had stood for many minutes, watching everything, her eyes lingering on Sarah's body. She hadn't shouted, hadn't screamed at Sarah or me, hadn't said a word until she turned around and left the room. I had known there was no use running after her. There was no use asking her to let me explain. There had been nothing to explain. Sarah had dressed quickly and then she too fled the house. The smell of shame had been heavy in the room. The smell lingered on the walls and on the windows.

I stepped into Isaac Street and trudged down the road. I walked past the beggar on a wheelchair who cried out for alms. I walked past the piss-stained wall of a business centre until I got to the Believers Today Assembly Church. Men in nice suits were hurrying into the church for the weekday service. For several minutes, I stood at the gate of the church staring at the sign: "Come unto me, all ye that labour and are heavy laden, and I will give you rest." I wasn't really much of a churchgoer, but I was curious about the kind of rest I could find in God's house. I pushed open the church door and stepped inside.

Yetunde had said many good things about this church: that

the founding pastor, Prophet Mark was "a great man of God," a "visionary leader" and a great "healing minister." The church members were singing:

Let your spirit come down
Let your spirit come down

I wondered if the spirit would possess me, if I would fall down under the anointing. I could certainly feel something in the air, but was it because the church had no proper ventilation? The brother beside me, a man clad in a faded suit, was convulsing, but no one paid any attention to him.

Holy angel of God, take control of my spirit
Holy angel of God, here I am at your feet
I surrender all
I surrender all

The congregation began praying loudly, but I did not fall under the anointing. Three people in front of me were twisting on the floor. Perhaps it was my sin holding me back, I thought. I was taught to believe that sin stood in the way between man and God. Sin caused the Holy Spirit to stay away from a brother or sister. I wanted to confess my sin, but where would I start?

Prophet Mark climbed the pulpit and took the microphone from the choir master. "This service will be different," the prophet announced. "We will pray for this country, for the Niger Delta. This is our home. It doesn't matter if we are just sojourners here on earth. We must banish the spirit of terrorism. We must chase away the spirit of strife, of conflict, of evil."

The congregation raised their voices, and the curses and rebukes flew out in all directions. Those in the business of trading asked the evil spirit to go away and never return.

"Get away from my business, you wicked forces. Pack your

load and never return to my household."

"Spirit of destruction, depart from my household! Go! Let me live in peace."

"You drinkers of blood, hear me today: you shall not see my blood to drink! May you die of thirst!"

"Turn to your neighbour and say it is finished," the prophet commanded.

The congregation obeyed. I did not move, but the man beside me did. "It is finished," the man screamed, spraying my face with spit.

The prophet urged the congregation to continue their prayers. He said that they were living in perilous and trying times. He asked them to open their bibles, where he read about the Lord's hands, ears and His separation from sinners.

The man preached, "That is God's message for you this day. That is his message of hope for you today. When you pray and feel that things are not working well for you, search within yourselves! Look around you. Your enemy might just be around the corner, planting evil seeds in your life."

"Praise the Lord!" someone cried.

The prophet's eyes darted around the people in the tiny church. I sat rigidly, my mouth wide open. I wondered if there were enemies at work in my life. Was Sarah an agent of the Devil? I wished I could feel better; I wished the shame of cheating would leave me alone. Would Yetunde forgive me?

The preacher's voice had become hoarse and sweat poured down his face. "Is your business failing and it seems there's no hope? Believe me, the Devil is at work. The word of God, the Bible, tells us that the Devil comes to steal, kill and destroy. But, by the special powers conferred on me, I will chase away misfortune from your household. Evil shall not be your lot. As long as you have stepped inside this building, you will be saved! Brethren, don't be deceived. God is not mocked, for whatsoever a man sows, so shall he reap!"

"Preach on, sir!" somebody called out.

Prophet Mark mopped his brow. "Our God is a merciful God. He is the same God who delivered the Israelites from the land of Egypt, the same God who parted the Red Sea, the same God who sent manna to the Israelites. He is the same yesterday, today and forever and He will deliver you from the hands of your enemy! But you must be born again. Is there a soul here who would want to ask God for forgiveness? Is there someone here who wants to be born again? I would encourage you to come up to the pulpit. Don't be shy. Come up. Come and have some rest!"

I shook my head. There was no way I was going to the front of the church. *The pastor and his members can have their rest*, I said to myself as I walked out.

I got to work very early the following day. When Boniface arrived, he took one look at my flushed face and then asked, "What is it?"

With a deep feeling of sadness, I told my friend and colleague how Yetunde had caught me pants down with the intern. To my annoyance, he laughed.

"The rule about infidelity is: don't be caught," he said. "You are free to have an affair, but don't be caught. I have many girlfriends. My wife will never catch me. God forbid."

"But I have been caught," I said. "What can I do?"

Boniface ran his hand over his head. "Yes, you have been caught and that is bad, but there must be a way. There's always a way."

For some minutes we considered the lies we could tell Yetunde: that Sarah had used juju on me. People said it was possible for small girls in Lagos to trap men with their love potions, but the chances of Yetunde believing such stories would be slim.

"Please, talk to her on my behalf," I begged Boniface. "She won't answer my calls."

"I will see what I can do. Meanwhile, what about Sarah?"

"I don't want to hear that name here!" I shouted. "I have gotten over her spells."

Boniface smiled and promised to call Yetunde. Two hours later, she agreed to see me at a restaurant in Ikoyi.

Yetunde was wearing a blue dress. I recognised it immediately as one from Beautiful Selections. A few heads in the restaurant turned to look at her. I felt like kissing the ground she walked on.

"Hi," I said.

She didn't respond. She didn't apologise for keeping me waiting for over an hour. She didn't even look at me, as she sat down.

"I can't believe I am sitting here beside you," she said. Her voice cracked. I felt the urge to touch her face, to kiss the strain away. I wanted her to look up.

"What would you like to drink?" I asked her.

Only then did she look up. But it was very brief. She didn't want to take anything from me, neither food nor drink. I ordered myself a non-alcoholic cocktail.

"Was she a good fuck?" she asked.

I almost choked. I had never heard her use such words before.

"I was good to you," Yetunde said. "I was faithful. I never wanted to be with another man. It never crossed my mind to cheat."

I repeated that I was sorry, but Yetunde shouted that I

wasn't, that I had shamed her, that I was a big fool. I swallowed nervously. I was happy there was no one seated near to us.

"I am sorry," I said. "Please forgive me. Please don't leave me."

Yetunde stood up abruptly. "I cannot forgive you. Never. I only came here to tell you that I want to come and collect my remaining things from your house. Good day."

She walked away. I stared at where she had been sitting and began to recall things about her, images that came to me suddenly. I remembered her collection of Rimmel London eye liners and how she religiously applied them every time she went to church. I remembered her food, the spices she added to the soups and stews. Most importantly, I remembered her dances, the way her body used to respond to music.

"Forget about her!" Boniface told me when I got back to the station. "Who does she think she is? You are not even married to her. You have begged her. What else does she want you to do? I beg of you, let me take you to a press conference so you can take your mind off this babe. Who knows, you might even see someone you admire there."

The press conference was in the Den club. The story of the Den was not complete without the story of Solomon.

Aged 25, Solomon had arrived at Lagos from the eastern part of Nigeria with a small portmanteau that contained his most prized possessions: his rosary and his carpentry tools. He had no formal education, but he had spent six years in his uncle's carpentry shed. Music had been what kept him going, what had fuelled him those long days when he was sawing and polishing wood. A man who loved to sing, he had been a member of an amateur choir, the Pure Evangelical Boys Band.

He established The Den which soon became the number

one hot spot for young people. It was one of the few clubs in the city that had a proper soundproof system. And there were enough parking spaces that could accommodate the expensive cars of the rich. As Solomon prospered, so did his friendships with women. They came from colleges, universities and the labour market to savour his sweet voice. Solomon liked the attention.

Solomon was a bit tipsy when Boniface and I arrived for the press briefing. Several journalists were also there. "I want you guys to have fun in my house," Solomon told us. "There shouldn't be any dull moments."

Two girls were at his side, both scantily dressed. One had her hand around Solomon's waist. "It is women that will kill this man," Boniface whispered to me.

"I want my song played on every radio station in this country," Solomon announced. "I want it played morning, afternoon and night. I want my song played all the time. You must declare my song number one in the charts!"

Solomon knew that this would cost him some money, but he did not mind. His manager had already packaged the brown envelopes for us journalists. "I have compiled a list of radio stations," the manager told us. "When I call out your station, please come out to collect your CD and the envelope."

He read out the names slowly and a representative of the station walked up to collect his envelope. Boniface went up to collect on behalf of Radio Sunrise. When the man had finished reading his list, a few people protested.

"You did not call my radio station," one man said.

"And what radio station is that?" the manager asked.

"Intercity FM," the man responded.

"Sorry. I have never heard of the station," the manager said.

"Are you saying my station does not exist?" The guy from

Intercity FM didn't wait for an answer to his question. He grabbed the manager and lifted him up. He was a huge fellow. I wondered if he was really a broadcaster.

"Put me down!" the manager screamed. "Put me down!"

Solomon's bodyguards came to the man's rescue. They hit the self-styled broadcaster until his grip on the manager loosened. "Get these stupid journalists out of this place," the manager told the bouncers. "I don't want to see any of them anymore. Drive them away!"

On our way back to the office, Boniface and I discussed the man from Intercity FM and how he had embarrassed us.

"He may not have been a journalist, you know," Boniface said, shaking his head.

"True," I responded. "We haven't even counted how much is in the brown envelope."

I brought out the money and counted the notes. It was 30,000 naira, but we would have to share the money with Ruth, the on-air personality, who would actually play the song on her shift.

Boniface tuned in to Radio Sunrise in time for the news. The presenter announced, "Here is the news. The Nigerian President, Umaru Yaradua has proposed an amnesty and unconditional pardon for militants in the Niger Delta in an effort to end years of attacks on Africa's biggest oil and gas industry. The government estimates that up to 20,000 militants could take part in the scheme. The government has said that the gunmen who surrender their arms will be given money and food allowances during the amnesty programme..."

I let out a cheer and Boniface almost lost control of the steering. We immediately began to debate the amnesty.

"Do you know why the government is doing this?" Boniface asked. "The truth is a lot of these militants have indicated that they are tired of fighting and want to get out of it."

"It is a good thing that the government is starting this amnesty," I said. "But will these militants really disarm? Will they really trust the government?"

"That's a good point," Boniface said, as he made a right turn. "Why should anyone trust the government? A government that says one thing but does another. Why should anyone trust it?"

"These militants have no choice," I responded. "If they don't surrender now, they will be caught later and it won't be funny at all."

We were still arguing when we walked into the premises of Radio Sunrise. Immediately I was told that Apollo Man had sent for me. My heart sank. I was sure he had found out about what had happened with Sarah. I wanted to face my dismissal bravely, but I was quaking.

"I am sure you are happy about the amnesty," he said to me as I entered his office.

"I am happy, sir," I responded warily.

"We pray for peace in Nigeria," Apollo Man said. "Anyway, I just wanted to thank you for mentoring the intern, Sarah. She's going back to the university today."

I wanted to laugh. Should I tell my boss about the wild sex I had with his niece? Should I tell him that the mentoring had cost me my relationship? I kept quiet.

"Well done," the boss said.

That night, I had a long talk with my parents. They were clearly pleased about the amnesty. "Our God is good," my mother said. "He answers prayers. Now, peace will reign in the land."

Everyone began to be hopeful that the amnesty really

would bring about peace. We began to look forward to the actual surrender of weapons. And with Boniface's help, I made another attempt to see Yetunde. My flat, where we had made love night and day, had suddenly become out of bounds to her. We met at a new restaurant in Victoria Island, a franchise of a London-based food chain. People said it was owned by a retired minister of the federal republic. I ordered seafood, but Yetunde refused to eat. "I didn't come here because I am hungry," she snapped.

I nibbled at my cold food. I would have preferred if we had met somewhere else. The portion was so small it made me want to cry. We used to say that if you took a girl on a date to The Lord Is My Shepherd Foods and she finished the meal, then that girl had enough appetite to eat up one's destiny.

"Yesterday, I was listening to a song about a fool in love," Yetunde said. "It dawned on me how much of a fool I have been."

In her text message, she had said she would do a lot of talking, that she had a lot on her mind, so I was prepared to listen.

"I trusted you," she continued. "I don't know why, but I did. Even when friends and colleagues said that you were no good, I still stayed."

Being "no good" meant a man didn't have a good car or enough money to treat a girlfriend. Some of Yetunde's colleagues took delight in dating married men who had come to be treated at the hospital. I had seen a few of these nurses, who looked more like vampires to me. It was an open secret that at least two nurses turned their white uniforms to seduction robes, because when the patients were rich, these nurses went that extra mile to help them recover quickly.

"I stayed by you because I loved you," Yetunde continued.

"Now my colleagues are laughing at me. How old is she?"

I dropped my cutlery. "Yetunde, please can we talk about us?"

"Us!" she screamed. "Were you thinking of us when you took the girl home to fuck her? Were you?"

A waiter hurried to our table. He wanted to know if everything was okay. The management didn't like trouble, he said. It was a respectable restaurant. Expatriates and diplomats regularly dined there.

"Everything is fine," I answered.

The waiter lingered a little before walking away. I wanted to fling my plate at the ugly man. I felt like telling him to take his small portions and shove them up his arse. Yetunde rummaged in her bag. She brought out a letter.

"I have had this letter for a while now," she told me. "It's an offer of employment in a US hospital. I never responded because I wasn't sure if I wanted to go. I didn't want to leave you. But now, I have said yes to the offer. I am leaving you. I am leaving Nigeria to work abroad."

She pushed the letter towards me, but I refused to touch it. My mind was sprinting. So Yetunde was going abroad. I knew there were agencies in Lagos that sorted out employment for Nigerian nurses in the US. In fact, I knew a certain barrister in my street who had helped more than fifty nurses rebuild their lives. Was he the one who was helping Yetunde?

"But you can't leave," I told her.

She laughed: a short maniacal burst that stung my ears. It wasn't the sort of laughter that I was used to. "I am leaving you for good," Yetunde said.

She stood up. I stood up. I wanted to stop her, but she shrugged my hands away. I brushed the tumbler and it fell to the floor and shattered. The waiter hurried to our table. Even before the man asked anything, I told him that everything was fine, as Yetunde walked out of the restaurant.

"Please, get me my bill," I told the waiter.

"What else did you expect?" Boniface asked me later. "She has told you it is over. Let her go. She is not the only fish in the river, you hear?"

But Yetunde was my only fish in the river. I had done my fair share of fishing. I had cast my net wide and caught the best in the seas. I wasn't ready to let go. On my way back from work, I drove over to her place. The gateman gave me a look that suggested all was not well. "Sule, is Yetunde at home?" I asked.

The gateman shook his head. "No, I have not seen her since yesterday."

At that moment a black Benz pulled up in front of the gate. Yetunde alighted from the passenger seat of the car. She took one look at me and her tongue was let loose: "What are you doing here? Get out! Don't let me ever see you here again. Sule, throw this fool out of my house!"

Sule, the man I had tipped many times, moved towards me. Sule, the man whom I often slipped 500 naira whenever I slept over at Yetunde's place, came over to me and with the same hand that he used to collect my tips, pushed me out of the compound.

I stopped shaving after Yetunde left me. The woman who used to stroke my clean-shaven chin was gone. Even my mother heard the despair in my voice when she called. I told her it was work-related stress and she went into a prayer session.

Chapter 14

As I was mourning the loss of Yetunde, the amnesty programme was taking shape in my country. Throughout the Niger Delta, the militants were surrendering their weapons in large numbers. Radio Sunrise reported the developments with keen interest. A reporter was assigned to follow the progress of events. In one of our news reports, we described the amnesty as "unprecedented in the history of armed struggle." Several ex-militants began undertaking a variety of educational courses across the country and the world. Some were sent for diving and underwater welding training in India. Others were sent by the government to South Africa, the UAE and Malaysia to acquire vocational skills, like learning how to fly planes. We wrote nice commentaries that were presented on air, but behind the scenes many of us spat fire.

"I don't know if it is such a good idea to send former freedom fighters to learn how to fly planes," Boniface said.

I did not reply and Boniface began to berate me. "What is the matter with you? I don't like the way you are behaving o! Maybe you need to go somewhere for a while. Have you spoken to your parents?"

I had a long chat with my mother, who had talked about the new five-star hotel that the government was building in Ibok. "It's a sight to behold," she had said. "And they've not even finished yet. What will it be like when it is finished? I thank the Lord for giving us a good leader."

There had been a spark in her voice. Something I had not heard in a while. Something that made me smile. My mother was happy. The peace in the land had made her happy. Why couldn't I be happy too? Why couldn't I move on, like Boniface said? Yetunde had made her decision. When I was through talking with my mother I went to bed and, for the first time in a long while, I slept soundly.

Apollo Man's office had been given a face lift. The ancient furniture that had been his office's companion for decades had been cleared out. Halleluyah! Radio Sunrise had struck a barter deal with Supreme Furniture. Rather than paying for airtime, which would have cost an arm and a leg, the company gave out their products. But a directive had arrived from the Director General's office that only senior members of staff should benefit from the deal.

"It is a wonderful thing," Apollo Man told me when I went to see him, "to sit on this chair. Let me tell you something. Last week, when the furniture arrived, the chairs were so comfortable I could not sit straight. Now my buttocks are getting used to it."

The smell of leather sickened me. Supreme Furniture had not said anything about the smell in their thirty second jingle that promised "a unique journey." We ran that jingle fifteen times a day.

"Sit down," the manager told me. "Experience this eighth wonder of the world. There is nothing in the circular that says that junior members of staff cannot sit here. Nothing at all. Just be careful, so you don't fall down. There's a small lever, something underneath that controls the position of the chair."

I lowered myself on the chair. Gently. Though the manager

had exaggerated, the chair was indeed comfortable. I let my hand wander underneath the chair to feel the lever, but didn't adjust the position.

"I have to be careful who sits on this chair," Apollo Man said. "I don't mind slim people like you but I'd prefer the likes of my secretary to bring her stool in here if she wants to have a meeting with me. Her massive weight may just destroy this beautiful furniture. I am sure the carpenters did not make this for obese people. The furniture did not come with manuals, you know. It would have been good to know about weight restrictions. But I will take precautions, just in case."

I knew that the adjustable furniture must have come with a manual. The manager, like most people, may have thrown it away. At Radio Sunrise, very few people read manuals.

"I don't even have to get up from my chair to take something out of my cupboard," Apollo Man continued. "I can wheel myself over there. Like this."

He glided across the room. He reminded me of someone I had seen earlier in Glover Road, skating on the pavement. But the skater was a teenager in tracksuit.

"Now, let's push this chair business aside," said the manager. "Let's talk about something that just came up." I listened as my boss told me about the amnesty programme for ex-militants, about rehabilitation for the boys. "A film training course has been set up for some ex-militants in Ibok," the manager explained. "I want you to go and do a documentary on it. Everything will be arranged for you: accommodation, transport and dining allowance. Think about it. Let me know by tomorrow."

It was all too much for me; it was all too sudden. I didn't particularly like the way things had turned out in my life. Yetunde was gone. I had messed around with an intern, but perhaps I could redeem myself by doing that documentary. Ibok was my hometown. It was where my mother and father lived. My cousin was the vice-chairman of the local council. A trip to Ibok would be an opportunity for me to clear my head and make some quick cash, as I could pocket the hotel allowance by staying with my parents. I told my boss that I was ready to go.

Boniface thought that I was one lucky chap. He considered it a rare privilege to be sent on such an assignment, especially to such a rich region. "Permit me to wish you a great fucking time!" Boniface exclaimed.

My face immediately tightened. I knew exactly what Boniface meant. A fucking time indeed! "Boniface, I don't like what you have just said."

But my colleague laughed it off and then launched into a story of a girl he once dated, a girl named Ime. "She had everything you could ever want," Boniface said. "She was well-endowed, if you know what I mean. Could cook like a pro. Could dance very well. And most importantly, was a tigress in bed. I looked forward to seeing her every night."

I took a sip of water. Someone had started to play music from his mobile phone, inside the canteen, and I immediately recognised the tune as one that Yetunde loved. Had my lover been a tigress? I enjoyed what I had with Yetunde. But what we did together stayed in the bedroom. I could never be crazy enough to describe it to friends or colleagues at work.

"Look, there is no need for you to take offence," Boniface said. "It's a known fact that the girls from your area are killers. It's a special gift from nature. No one can deny it. It's been five years since I was with Ime, but I still think of what she did to me."

I looked at my watch. It was half past four: time to leave.

I had a lot to sort out before the trip. Boniface gave one last warning, "Whatever happens, please don't forget to use a condom!"

Chapter 15

"They have sacked Boniface!" I was told the next morning as I walked past the security gate. A new intern, Tolu, was the harbinger of the evil news. She was standing with the gateman, her bag slung over shoulder. I stopped. "What did you say?"

"They have sacked Boniface," Tolu repeated, pleased that she had found an attentive listener. "It happened this morning. As Boniface entered the office, they gave him one white envelope. Boniface thought it was money. But when he opened it, he screamed. I have never heard any person scream like that in this place."

I got full details of the story in the office. Boniface had opened up *News Personality of the Week*, a live news programme, to phone callers. A mischievous caller had said some unpalatable things about the president of the country. Radio Sunrise's staff huddled together in small groups, discussing Boniface's fate. Some people believed Boniface shouldn't have been sacked; it wasn't his fault that someone said something silly on the phone. Others felt the presenter had been foolish and hadn't behaved like a trained Nigerian broadcaster.

"Why didn't he cut the call?" someone asked. "Has he forgotten that this is a government radio station?"

"Point of correction," another interjected. "It is a public radio station."

"Does that give people the permission to call in and insult

the government? Do they think this is the BBC where people can phone in and insult the prime minister?"

"But if he had cut the call," someone pointed out, "people would know who cut it. That to me would have been a greater embarrassment to the government."

"Are you an amateur broadcaster? Don't you know how to cut a call nicely and pretend that you lost connection, eh?"

If the management of Radio Sunrise had thought that they had heard the last of Boniface, they were mistaken. Four hours after he was fired, his family arrived at the station with a bishop. When they were prevented from seeing the director, Boniface's wife sat on the floor.

"I will sit here and wait," the woman said.

The preacher brought out the contents of his bag: a Bible, a bottle of anointing oil and a holy handkerchief. He began to sing and pray loudly with Boniface's family. At half past six, the director emerged from his office and walked towards his car. Boniface's family members rushed at the man and fell flat on the ground where he stood.

"I beg you in the name of God," Boniface's wife began. "Do not fire my husband. He is the one that feeds us all…"

"God will bless you, sir. It will forever be well with you," the preacher said. "No misfortune shall befall your family. Wealth shall remain with you always."

When the youngest member of the group, a young girl of about four years, bent down and kissed the man's shoes, the director sighed. He said Boniface would be reinstated. The family let out a loud cheer. The preacher began to pour blessings on the director: "You will never lack. Your children will never lack. Your children's children will never lack."

I turned to Helen, one of the newsreaders who, like the other staff in Radio Sunrise, had come out to witness the drama. I could smell her perfume, something slightly overpowering that made me think of incense. My eyes traced the curves of the lady's body. Some people were born lucky. How else could someone explain how a woman in her fifties could remain so fit?

"The way the director ranted about the phone-in programme," the woman said, "I would have thought that that was the end of Boniface. But…" She raised her hand in exasperation.

The woman's cavilling was of no interest to me; I was happy Boniface had been reinstated.

"Ours is a society populated by beggars," Helen continued. "A man steals public funds and when he is caught, he goes on a begging spree. Then he is forgiven, just like that. No chastisement. Nothing."

Chastisement. A word I thought was used for children, for delinquents. A word which for many months hadn't danced near to my ears.

"How is your girlfriend?" the woman suddenly asked.

"Well…"

The woman smiled. "You think I don't know what you young boys are up to in this office? You think I don't know about your affairs with all the small girls that come here on internships?"

I hurried away from her.

Chapter 16

I travelled to the Niger Delta with Anders Star Air via the Calabar airport. Our studio manager at Radio Sunrise said that the proprietor of Anders Star Air was a devout Christian, unlike some other diabolical transporters who engineered plane crashes, so they could "suck the victims' blood." "Children of the Devil" the man called these blood suckers. He still subjected me to a prayer session, to ward off every evil in the air.

The woman sitting next to me on the plane had the physique of a model, like one of those who graced the covers of the many lifestyle magazines that had flooded Lagos recently. Before boarding, I had prayed for a nice travelling companion, someone who would mind his or her business. During my last air travel, I had had the misfortune of sitting beside an oil worker. The man had suffered from verbal diarrhoea. He had boasted of his numerous trips to Europe and America, the five star hotels he lodged in and the women who came with the travelling lifestyle. I noticed my travelling companion's *Cosmopolitan* and *Hello* and was pleased. The magazines ought to keep her company. But five minutes after the plane had taken off, the lady turned towards me and asked, "Are you going home?"

"Pardon?"

She smiled. "You are flying to Calabar. Are you from there?"

"No. I am on my way to Ibok."

"I hear Calabar is a wonderful city, but I am actually going to Obudu cattle ranch."

Most of us in Lagos had heard about the ranch. In the region, it was the only tourist resort that could be regarded as world class. It had everything: canopy walk, cable cars and a presidential helipad. Its sporting complex was complete with floodlit tennis courts and fully-equipped gymnasium.

"It's an ideal place to rest," the lady said. "I have not had a holiday in five years."

The fact is, although the lady looked fit, the lines on her face suggested that she was not exactly a spring chicken.

"I have colleagues who go abroad every year on holidays," she said. "But they would never go to anywhere in Nigeria. In fact, I used to be like that. But this year, I made a resolution to be a patriotic Nigerian."

She wore no ring, I realised. Did it mean that she was single? She was certainly a top earner. Not many Nigerians could afford travelling abroad on holidays.

The woman folded her magazines and fixed her full attention on me. My heart sank.

"I have heard so much about Calabar," she said. "My brother used to work there. He told me about the food, the music, the dance and of course the women. When he returned to Lagos, he came back with a Calabar girl."

Her brother, she said, started a family war. No-one from the Adeleke clan had married a non-Yoruba. Her mother threatened fire and thunder, saying she would rather be shot dead than consent to the marriage. The father promised to disinherit him, to strike out his name from the will. It made no difference to Tunde, who had always been stubborn; love further fortified his stubbornness.

"For over a year, my parents did not talk to Tunde," the lady revealed, "but he stood his ground. They got married last month. It shamed me, the way my mum danced at the wedding; the same woman that wanted to kill herself because of the girl. But it taught me something. It taught me that love conquers all."

To my dismay, beads of perspiration appeared on my forehead. Why would a stranger open up to me that way? Was the family the famous Adelekes? The ones who owned the Almond Bank?

Just when I thought the lady had decided to go back to her magazines, she continued, "I dated an Ibo man in Lagos. An intelligent and very handsome man who wanted to marry me. I loved him. I wanted to be with him, but I was scared of what my parents would say, what they would do. The man waited for me to make up my mind, to say yes to his proposal. But I couldn't. I was a coward. So he went away."

I shifted on my seat, opened my mouth and the words flew out: "My girlfriend just left me. It's not a very nice thing to happen to a guy, especially when you have been with the girl for a long time."

The lady gave me a sympathetic look. "You poor thing! Why would any woman want to leave a cute guy like you? Do you want to talk about it? I am happy to listen."

It was not the expected response. I leaned closer to the woman, close enough to see the acne that the brown powder had tried so hard to cover up. "Who are you?" I asked.

The lady kept smiling. There was something beneath the smile. Something charming, yet troublesome. "Why do you want to know who I am?" she asked.

"I am a journalist. I like to know things."

Perhaps I should not have mentioned my profession. The

word "journalist" seemed to make some women in Lagos immediately take to their heels. But it sparked off something in my travel companion.

"A journalist?" she exclaimed. "I studied media at university, but my father wouldn't let me go into broadcasting. He felt it was a profession that had no financial prospects, but I have always respected broadcasters."

Her father was right, I told her. There was no fianancial fulfilment in the profession. Most broadcasters could not afford holidays in America or Europe. They could not even afford to fly down for a weekend in Obudu.

"But money is not everything," she said. "So many bankers have money, but they are not happy."

So she was a banker. She must really be from the Adeleke family. It was a real privilege sitting beside her.

"Obi used to work in a radio station," she said.

"Who?"

"My Ibo boyfriend. He was an on-air personality. I looked forward to hearing his voice every night. He always sent me coded wishes. Sometimes he read poems, love poems that caressed me through the air."

When we landed at Calabar, we exchanged cards. I quickly read hers: "Funke Adeleke, Head of Corporate Affairs, Almond Bank." I promised to keep in touch.

Chapter 17

"Shall we pray?" the driver enquired before we started the one-hour journey from the Calabar airport to Ibok. The driver prayed for safety, for guidance and for an extra pair of eyes to see the Devils that might confuse him on the road. He prayed for special skills to dodge the treacherous potholes.

"You think it will be better today?" the driver asked me as the car danced along the uneven road.

I turned towards the man. "What?"

"The traffic," the driver responded. "It was horrible yesterday. I spent six hours on this road. The same road that normally I spend sixty minutes on."

Six hours! It had taken me less than an hour to fly from Lagos to Calabar. The driver explained that the traffic was caused by road construction awarded to an incompetent indigenous building company. The state government had said something about developing local business talent; they had used the media to broadcast their message of "local jobs for local people."

"I don't have a problem about indigenous people fixing our roads," the driver said. "But let it be competent people. Let the right person do the right job. What does a philosopher know about road construction?"

As we passed the construction workers, I noticed a man in blue coverall and wondered if he was a graduate of philosophy.

Perhaps his father or uncle owned the indigenous construction company. Then the potholes that had swallowed large parts of the road came into full view.

"It is the wicked rains that destroy our roads," the driver explained to me. "Whenever it rains you would think the heavens are angry. That is why experts should be the ones who fix our roads. People who understand the weather and the topography of the area. Not some philosophy graduate who is a relative of the governor."

The driver was probably a university graduate. He was one of the many young men who left the university with so much hope, but ended up earning a living in ways they had never imagined.

When we came to a police roadblock, a young policewoman walked up to the vehicle, her gun hanging on her broad shoulders. She peered into the car and smiled.

"What's in your boot?" she asked the driver.

"Nothing," the driver responded.

"Let me see it," the policewoman said.

The driver grumbled as he alighted from the car and walked over to the boot, closely followed by the policewoman.

"But you said there was nothing in the boot," she said when she saw my luggage in the boot.

"It's only a small bag," the driver replied.

"But it is something," the policewoman responded. "You said there was nothing inside the boot. You lied to me. That's an offence."

I knew the police could escalate the incident, could delay us at the checkpoint and could ask the driver for his birth certificate or his tax receipt. These sorts of scenes occurred over and over in Lagos. I stepped out of the car.

"Please, accept my apologies," I told the police officer. "I guess the driver misunderstood your question. We are just coming from the airport. The bag in the boot is mine."

The policewoman stared at me. Her eyes roamed my face, my starched shirt and skinny trousers. Her eyes lingered on my shoes. They were Chelsea boots. Well-polished, they glistened in the sun. I had purchased them from Igwe, one of the official drivers at Radio Sunrise who often smuggled contraband goods from Cotonou.

"I like the way you dress," the policewoman told me. "For this reason, I will allow you to go. I will not arrest the driver. But he should be truthful next time. Don't lie to a police officer."

"That's a first," the driver said when he drove off. "I have never seen a police officer let someone go because he is well-dressed. Never heard of it. You must be a blessed fellow."

I stayed silent because I didn't want to be dragged into some self-indulgent discourse on piety. My ears were not ready to hear those familiar lines: "God is in control."

The car swerved as the driver dodged another pothole.

"The police have no reason to mount road blocks on the highway," the driver said. "It should be illegal. What are they checking, anyway?"

Again, he got no response from me. I however told the driver to stop when we approached some roadside stalls. The traders sold everything from bush rat to giant snails. A large fish caught my eye.

"How much is that?" I asked without stepping out of the car. Suddenly traders surrounded the car, confusing me with their jumble of cries.

"Buy my fish: it's the best in the world!"

"I will give you a good bargain!"

"My fish is very delicious! You will not regret it!"

I bought the catfish that had caught my eye in the first

place. It was the sort of fish that my mum would appreciate. The sort that would thicken her pot of stew.

The gas flare welcomed me to Ibok. Our big red scar that would not go away. Every year, the oil companies operating in my community and the government said they were discussing how to reduce flares. These discussions had started during my secondary school days. My father used to be a member of a committee set up by the government and the oil companies to "look into the matter." He used to attend meetings most Saturdays at the townhall, which bordered the Comprehensive Secondary School, his alma mater. Often times, he would come back home fuming and cursing the oil companies: "These people are playing with our lives! God will judge them!" He quit the committee when I got into the university because all the Saturday discussions had led nowhere. Our big red scar simply refused to go away.

Ibok, my hometown, my place of birth, the land of yellow soil and plentiful palm trees, was a small town of many bungalows. The tallest building was only three storeys high. We drove past rows of bungalows covered in yellow dust, past children and young women with mountains of firewood on their heads. The only time my family cooked with firewood was during Christmas, when my father slaughtered a goat and roasted it outside. But I had never gathered firewood by myself. I was a privileged child. My mother cooked with clean, burning gas.

The driver turned into Uruk Road and then my family house stood out among the other rows of bungalows, because it was fenced and gated with black iron. The tree that was planted when I was five years old had shed all its leaves and stood with its naked branches sticking up.

My mother was the first person to rush out and welcome me. "Welcome, my dear! Did you have a nice journey?"

I hugged her. "Yes, Mummy, I did." Her dress smelled of spices and palm oil.

I took my luggage from the car, paid the taxi driver, then went straight inside the kitchen to deposit the fish. It was obvious that my mother still used the same old cooker despite the fact that I had sent her money a long time ago to buy a new one.

"I gave the money to the church," my mother informed me. "God's house must be completed first. The Bible warns us that we should not live by bread alone. Besides, what is wrong with my cooker, eh?" Her attention switched to the fish. "Why didn't you tell me that you were bringing fish? I have already used stockfish to prepare the soup."

"Sorry, Mummy, I am sure you can use the fish to make pepper soup the way I like it."

My mother smiled. "Trust me. I will make you the best pepper soup you have ever eaten."

I embraced my father in the living room. Oh, how frail my father had become! The dress he wore, the long-sleeved shirt hung on his body like a curtain draped over a scarecrow. Was he sick? Was it just old age? He looked so different from the man in the picture hanging above the bookshelf.

"Let us pray," my father said, later when we gathered around the dining table. He prayed slowly, enunciating every word. He thanked God for His kindness, His mercies, for bringing me home back safely.

"Our father and our God, we thank you for journey mercies. We thank you because you are still God. Your child has returned safely; we give you thanks. I commit him into your mighty hands. I cover him with the blood of Jesus. I command every evil eye that is watching him to be blind. No evil bird shall hover near his roof. No evil cat shall cry by his ears. What he has come to do, he shall accomplish. He will return in good health. He will prosper. He shall bear fruits. In Jesus' name, Amen."

I had almost forgotten how different my mother's food tasted, how she used very little pepper because of my father's stomach, how the garri was almost as hard as the chicken bone on his plate.

"I have missed your cooking, Mummy," I said.

My mother smiled. "I know someone who can cook well for you. A very beautiful girl who would make a good companion for you." She spoke these words as smoothly as if she had rehearsed a script.

In my family, such topics were rarely brought up at dinner tables. I put my cutlery down very quietly. My mother looked down and my father coughed, then steered the conversation away from the matter of the girl.

"You say your office sent you here to do a documentary on militants?" my father asked.

"Ex-militants," I responded.

"Don't they have people here who would do so?" my mother asked.

For the second time that day, I briefed my family on my peculiar assignment. From the way they looked at me, from the way my father nodded his head, it was obvious that they were impressed. My father's eyes seemed to say: "This is my beloved son with whom I am well-pleased."

After the meal, while Mum was in the kitchen, I went to sit with my father on the veranda. The old man enjoyed sitting on his raffia chair after a sumptuous meal. His theory was that the cool evening breeze made his food digest better.

"I am happy you are happy in Lagos," my father said. "I am pleased that you are doing a job that you enjoy. Many people have left for Lagos, but they never made it. Men like your aunt's husband. I do not understand such a man. He is still searching for gold in Lagos, you know."

My auntie Eno had, much to the chagrin of family members, married a loquacious fellow who claimed to be a qualified lawyer, but had never practiced even for one day. The man had never made a serious attempt at getting to court. My auntie painstakingly provided for him and their five children from her meagre teacher's earnings. In recent years, some people in my family started to believe the phoney lawyer had bewitched her. Then one day, he had left for Lagos in search of greener pastures. My auntie had not seen him in six months.

"He can easily get a job in Lagos," I said firmly. "Lawyers are in demand."

"He will not get a job there," my father replied. "He is too lazy, my son. Men like that should be shot, God forgive me. And your wife, Ifiok, when will we get to meet her?"

I almost choked. "Daddy..."

A smile appeared on my father's face. "Soon. Let it be soon, Ifiok. Let your soon be now. It is not a good thing to wait for too long before you marry. Or have you married a foreign woman and you do not want to tell us?"

"Daddy!"

He smiled. "It is not a bad thing. Just let us know and we will welcome her here. You know it will be nice for you to have a foreign wife like Paul."

Our former neighbour, Paul, was now the principal of State College. He had studied in the United States, then when he returned to Nigeria, he did so with his American wife, Shirley.

"Please be careful now that you are in Ibok," my father

advised. "They say there's peace in the land. I do not know about that. I would just ask you to be careful. The world is an evil place. You are my only child, please be careful. I am getting old, so I think it is time to pass on my knowledge to you. I would like you to know about my businesses and other matters related to the family so that when I am dead, you can take over."

My heart began to race. I didn't like these talks on death and had never really been involved in my father's affairs.

"Tomorrow," my father continued, "I would like us to visit the tenants in my house at Father's Lodge. They have arranged a meeting. You will learn about mediation. It would be like a rite of passage for you. You are not a boy anymore. You are a man."

In Ibok, rites of passage marked times of new beginning and transition from one phase to another, a move from childhood to adulthood. Sometimes, the rites involved an element of endurance and some physical test. Young men were taught to be brave and endure pain without complaint. It was all part of growing up.

In my room, I opened one of the boxes where my childhood photos were stored. It was some kind of ritual for me. Some of the photos were of my early years, when polaroid cameras performed wonders, like the one where I wore a blue cap and smiled at the camera, showing the gaps in my teeth. There were other pictures in the box that made me giggle, like the photo of my mother dressed in hot pants. My mother didn't even wear trousers anymore. In the church to which she belonged, it was considered a sin. The resident pastor always made sure the women in his congregation did not follow the ways of the world by painting their faces as well as wearing wigs or trousers. I was about to close the box when some voices floated from the living room. A stranger's voice was protesting, "But he is my son too!"

My mother responded, "How is he your son? Did you carry him for nine months in your belly? Please go, my son is sleeping. You can come back later."

Who is this woman? I wondered as I left my bedroom and approached the living-room. The female visitor rushed to hug me. "See my son! See how he has grown!" she cried.

She looked vaguely familiar. Her dress smelt of camphor. I looked to my mother to introduce the visitor.

"This is Edima, my distant relative. I am not sure you will remember her."

The visitor gasped. "Distant relative? I am your mother's second cousin. It is so good to see you, my son. The last time I saw you, you were only a boy."

"Now that you have seen him," my mother said firmly, "you can leave so the boy can rest. Can't you see he is tired?"

"He doesn't look tired to me," Edima argued. "These young men are never tired. You know, Mfon, my oldest son, he..."

"We can talk about your son later," my mother interrupted. "Please let my own son rest."

Edima's worn out shoes, her old blouse and her bony neck caught my attention. I took out a few notes from my pocket.

"Auntie, I didn't really bring much when I was coming, but you can have..."

Before I could complete my sentence, my mother snatched the money from my hands, giving the visitor only a few of the notes.

"God will bless you," the woman thanked me. "God will keep you safe from harm!"

"Amen!" my mother responded as she walked the visitor

to the door.

"Mummy, what was that about?" I asked when the woman was gone.

"If you give her all the money, what will you give the other people when they visit?" she said.

I shook my head and went back to my room to put a call through to Boniface.

"How is Ibok?" he asked. "Have you started recording yet?"

I laughed. "I just got into town. I will start recording in the next few days. For now, I am just enjoying my family."

Chapter 18

I awoke with the feeling that there was something in the air around me. A dog started barking in the distance, a nearer dog joined in and soon all kinds of animals began to perform a torturous symphony. My mother entered the room without knocking to ask me to pray with her. Goodness! I might have been prancing the room with my thing swinging like a pendulum.

After kneeling in prayer, she left and I went to the bathroom to find that the water was cold. My mother banged on the bathroom door and screamed, "Don't stay too long in there. Your breakfast will get cold."

That morning, I was shadowing my father during his meeting with his tenants at Father's Lodge, one of the low cost houses he owned. The property was what people called a "face-me-I-face-you" house. It had ten rooms for ten tenants who shared toilets and kitchens. The main kitchen in the lodge, the one fitted with a non-functional sink, was next door to the oldest tenant's room. It was there that the more affluent tenants, those with gas cookers and kerosene stoves, prepared their food. The other makeshift kitchen, made of old zinc, was erected outside beside the pawpaw tree.

"They said I should come and settle a small matter," my father said. "I hope it really is a small matter. Last time I was called to settle a bitter fight."

I hoped there wouldn't be another one.

The tenants were already seated on the chairs they had dragged outside when we arrived at the property. Some of them were fidgeting. My father did a quick introduction and a few of the tenants remembered me.

"He is now a man!" Edem exclaimed as he shook my hands. Edem was the one who had convened the meeting because he was alarmed about a new tenant called Johnny. Of course, Johnny had not been invited to the meeting.

"Have you seen the way he walks?" Edem asked the other tenants. "He is too polished, that man. I know his type. I know just what he has on his mind. I have two sweet daughters. Two sweet daughters that can easily fall under the spell of Mr Johnny. He is not good for this place, that man. He will pollute our erstwhile sanctity."

My journalism course included a module on conflict resolution. The veteran broadcaster Joe Odunsi who taught the class had often said, "Never be confrontational when you are out gathering news!" He had taught us about resolving conflicts within the context of news gathering, about reporting from dangerous spots like Oshodi or Mushin, but he had taught me nothing about how to resolve conflicts with neighbours or troublesome tenants. My father nodded his head at Edem, then turned to me and whispered, "To be a good judge, one must be a good listener."

"Oga, landlord, I am not happy that this man has moved in here," Edem said. "He should be asked to leave."

There was no law, I was sure, that gave tenants power to decide who should live with them. I knew a little about tenants' rights and the obligations of landlords.

"Oga, landlord, I have lived in this compound for over ten years," Edem declared. "I think I deserve to be treated fairly."

Another tenant, Udofia, suddenly stood up. "I am sick and tired of this whining! Edem, how can you feel threatened by Johnny? Look, all you need to do is talk to your daughters about sex education. Simple."

"It is your own daughter that you will teach sex education!" Edem retorted.

Udofia smiled. "Sex education is not a bad thing. I will gladly teach your daughters sex education, if you let me."

Edem waved a finger at Udofia. "I don't want to hear anymore of this nonsense. I invited the landlord here so that he can find a way to evict Mr Johnny. Let us discuss the matter at hand."

"But that is what we are doing," Udofia said. "We are discussing the matter in a scientific way. We must teach our young people sex education. They have a right to know what sexual intercourse is."

To my dismay, Edem and the other tenants began to argue. They exchanged hot words that charged up the already heated day. As the arguments went on, it became clear to me and my father that Johnny's eviction was not supported by the majority.

My father cleared his throat. "I understand your fears, Edem. But don't you think we should give Johnny the benefit of doubt? Let us remember that he is not from this community. Ibok people are loving people. We must welcome him first with love. If he throws back our love, then we will tell him that we are not a foolish people. In fact, I will personally come here to throw his things out. But let us give him a chance first."

"You have spoken well," Udofia said and others murmured their agreement. "That is what we will do."

Edem knew he had lost the fight. He let out a very long hiss. I wished I had some of my father's wisdom; his judgement would not be contested. I wished that I felt something, anything, rather than the numbness that engulfed me. But it was difficult to turn a brown-envelope collecting journalist into a mediator or acting landlord. Some irons are just too rigid to be bent.

"Next time, you will represent me," my father said, as we drove away.

When the car approached Bank Road, we stopped so I could get some cash from a bank. Someone had told me that the ATM machines that had sprouted all over the town were not to be trusted. They could swallow customers' cards at will. And it would take the grace of God to retrieve the card in five working days.

"Yes, your slip?" the teller asked me when it was my turn in the queue.

From her accent, I could tell that she was from the western part of Nigeria. I smiled at her and said a few words in Yoruba. The girl beamed.

"Ifiok, are you aware that you can upgrade your account," she said when she checked my account. "We have chequing accounts tailored to suit your needs. Deposits of cash and cheques are allowed. Other transactions include funds transfer, withdrawal, request for managers' cheques and several others. The good thing is that you will receive a monthly statement."

The teller did not say anything about charges, those hidden in very small prints that hurt the eyes. Some of my colleagues at Radio Sunrise who used such banking services always complained of small monthly deductions from their accounts.

"You can also take control of your account from anywhere you find yourself," the banker continued. "Use our twenty-four-hour telephone banking service, available free of charge to all our customers. From any telephone simply dial…"

I shook my head and interrupted her, "I am not interested."

She wouldn't let go so easily. She pushed leaflets at me. "International Connection provides you a most convenient online access to your account information so you can manage your money when you want it and how you want it. With the internet, you can connect to the bank whenever you want to and perform a variety of transactions."

"I am not some oil worker or a thieving politician," I said. "I am an ordinary government worker."

"It doesn't matter," the banker responded. "We cater for all classes of people. Perhaps you may be interested in our SMS banking service that allows you access to basic banking transactions through your mobile phone. With this service you can access your account any time. This is basically putting your bank in your hands."

Why was the woman troubling herself? Couldn't she tell from my clothes that I was not a rich man? I managed to leave the bank without signing up for any of the services.

"I never go to these new banks," my father said, when I got to the car. "I prefer my old and trusted Elephant Bank, where I know my money is safe."

"Daddy, your money can be safe too in these other banks," I told him.

My father's laughter was the sort that suggested that he did not agree with his son. He reminded me about the wonder banks of the eighties, about how they had all come up with mouthwatering offers to lure customers.

"I know people who died of heart attacks," he said. "People who were fooled by the offers. A pensioner had deposited all he had in one of these banks and then everything disappeared into thin air. Everything. The poor man just fell asleep. He never woke up."

I appreciated my father's warnings. When we got home,

another of my distant relatives was at the gate.

"I have been waiting here all day," he announced as he embraced me. "See the man you have become!"

Before my father could do the introductions, even before he could invite the man inside, the distant relative had started asking for money. "My daughter is very sick. I have been to the hospital. They need 50,000 naira before she can be treated. I do not have that kind of money. Please, my son, help me with the money. God will bless you. God will take away sickness from your household."

I gave the relative some money. The man prostrated himself to thank me.

When he left, my father said, "My son, don't believe all these stories you are hearing. Don't throw away all your money on these villagers."

Chapter 19

I remembered an old story about our people being fishermen with a river rich with fish, when we gathered at the dining table over a meal of fish stew. It was a story my mother told me when I was a boy. A story her own mother used to tell her. My mother had prepared the meal with her imported spices. Her good friend, Anna, travelled regularly to the US. Whenever she returned, she brought back packets of condiments with funny names like "Uptown Flavour," "Vitalising Power" and "New Moon." Because my mother was adventurous in her cooking, she tried them all.

"This tastes really nice," I said.

My mother smiled. "I am happy you like it."

"Really nice," I said. "You must give me some of your spices to take back with me to Lagos."

"What you need, darling, is a wife," my mother responded. "Cooking comes naturally to women. Let your wife do the cooking and worrying for you."

The food in my mouth suddenly tasted like foam. Why couldn't my mother stop talking about me getting a wife?

"Your mother is right, you know," my father added. "You are not a boy anymore. You are a man. We want you to settle down and have a family. Now is the time." Clearly he saw marriage as another rite of passage for me.

"Time is not on our side," my mother pleaded. "We are

getting old. We want to carry our grandchild before we die."

It was difficult swallowing the piece of fish in my mouth. This pressure was about being called a grandmother or grandfather. It was about their satisfaction, not mine.

"Mummy, are you trying to force me to get married?" I asked.

"We are encouraging you to get married," my mother responded. "In fact we have a perfect woman for you. Do you remember my friend Dorothy? Her daughter Idara is just..."

My knees felt weak. It was bad enough that they wanted me to get married very quickly, but the idea of them choosing a wife for me made my stomach churn.

"Where are you going?" my father asked.

"Daddy, I need to get some fresh air," I said, heading towards the door.

"You have not finished your food," my mother said. "Are you hot? We can put on the air conditioner."

"I will be back shortly."

I walked right out of the gate into the street. Perhaps my parents thought me incapable of approaching a lady. Oh, what manner of thinking!

My anger wouldn't subside so I decided to visit my cousin Ubong, the vice-chairman of Ibok Local Council. I would go to his office as I knew he often worked late. I had left my wallet behind so taking a motorbike taxi was out of the question. On the streets, I walked past many young women in miniskirts and tight jeans, similar outfits to what was seen on the streets of Lagos.

At Ubong's office, we hugged each other and he then immediately offered me iced tea and biscuits.

"You should have let me send my driver to come pick you up!" Ubong exclaimed, shaking his plump finger at me. "How could you have walked so far in this heat?"

For a man of thirty, being the executive vice-chairman of the local government was no small feat. Ubong's position came with all the benefits attached to political office holders: official car, driver, accommodation and frequent overseas trips.

Twenty years ago, every weekday, Ubong and I used to walk three times the distance to school. I wanted to remind him of that. I wanted to tell him that I enjoyed walking, that it was good for the body, but I drowned my words with the cold drink.

"People like you ran off to Lagos, thinking this town would never develop," Ubong said. "But look at us now. And this is just the beginning. People like us stayed behind to build this city, to make it like Lagos, better than Lagos even."

This was the same Ubong who couldn't pass his final exams in secondary school, the same person who ran to me whenever the English teacher gave us an assignment and the same person who had been suspended in class 4 because he was caught cheating. This same person had become a deputy leader of the local government.

"You could come and work for me as press secretary," Ubong offered as he sank heavily into his well-padded chair.

Every politician in the country had a press secretary or a media assistant to boost his image and his ego in the *Daily Times* or some other newspaper in the country. Some of the so-called press secretaries were inept reporters who had never cut their teeth in a newsroom. We liked to call them errand boys.

"Did I tell you I was looking for a job?" I retorted. "I have a job to do here in Ibok: to do a documentary on ex-militants."

"That's a very noble job," Ubong responded, nodding his balding head. "And very timely too. This region was falling apart. I am really happy peace has returned to Ibok. As a politician, I have dealt with all kinds of criminals, from petty thieves to armed robbers, but these militants, these boys from the creeks of the Niger Delta, make government laughable. My job was on the line. I really thank the good Lord for amnesty. If not for amnesty, you and I would not be talking here right now."

"So these militants had sophisticated guns?" I asked.

"It's not about the guns," my cousin, the politician said. "It's the juju that they use with the weapon. My bodyguard is a trained marksman. No criminal survives his bullets. Do you know he once shot a militant, but nothing happened to him? He brushed the bullets away like they were dewdrops."

It was only feeble minds like Ubong who believed in juju. It was the likes of Ubong who went in search of seers and witchdoctors to perform all kinds of rituals so they could stretch out their political tenures.

The door opened and a young girl in miniskirt entered the room. She walked over to Ubong and whispered to him.

"Tell them to wait!" Ubong shouted and waved the girl away. The lady deliberately swayed her hips as she walked away. She was one of Ubong's many personal assistants.

"That girl reminds me of someone I met on the plane," I said.

Ubong's face lit up. "Was she hot? Did you get her number?"

I was no stranger to politicians' insatiable appetite for women. We journalists gossiped about a senator who kept an album of Nigerian female celebrities and employed a personal assistant to chat with them on his behalf. Those who could quench the senator's thirst were rewarded with cash and contracts.

When I pulled the business card out of my pocket, Ubong snatched it, then smiled widely.

"Funke Adeleke!" Ubong exclaimed. "Oh my God, you

lucky bastard! She's a celebrity. I have seen her several times in magazines. I must call her! I have heard so much about her affairs."

Right under my nose, Ubong put in a call to Funke. My cousin used his practised charm. His voice was as sweet as sugar as he told her that she was a real beauty and would like to meet her. Was she still in Calabar? he wanted to know. Would she be able to come over to Ibok? The lady said she could come over to Ibok. Then they ended the conversation and my cousin winked at me.

I told Ubong about the conversation I had earlier with my parents and he patted me on the back.

"I have wanted to talk to you about this," he said. "You are not a boy anymore. You are a man now. You should be married. Look at me now. I have two kids. Are we not the same age? Did we not grow up together?"

I swallowed hard. This wasn't the expected response.

"You are an only child," Ubong continued. "You are your father's right-hand man. You are his heir. A lot is expected of you. Please, my brother, get married. Settle down and be a man. It doesn't stop you from having flings here and there. It's allowed in our society. Do you know how many girlfriends I have? But I am happily married with two kids. It's allowed."

His lecture did not make sense to me. Ubong was a man who said he was happily married, yet he was a philanderer with society's permission. "You must think about it very carefully," Ubong continued. "But you need to act fast."

His driver took me home. In the air-conditioned saloon, I wondered if it was a mistake returning to my hometown to do the documentary. The conversations around rites of passage to manhood would not have come up in Lagos. No one would have brought up such discussions over the phone.

"You are back," my mother said.

There was something in the voice that made my legs weaken. Oh, my poor mother! A million and one of her good deeds went through my mind. It was clear that she meant well. She loved me. I sat down beside her.

"Mummy, your friend's daughter, do you know her well?"

My mother looked at me in bemusement for a moment, then spoke rapidly, "She is a very good girl, I can tell you that. Very respectful. Very homely. Very beautiful. And she can cook very well."

Those were the qualities that traditional Ibok men sought in their women. When my father came to join us, he assured me, "We are only looking after you. That's our responsibility as parents. Please, my son, consider our request. Just see the girl first." He patted my hand. "If you don't like her, there won't be any problem."

Chapter 20

My mother drove the short distance to NEPA Estate where the Akpans lived. I was bemused by how many abandoned and uncompleted houses littered the neighbourhood. Mum explained that once upon a time the god of prosperity had smiled upon the community. But one day the Devil came like a thief in the night and reversed their fortunes.

When my mother pulled up in front of our destination, I was relieved that the house was completed and painted in bright colours. Mrs Akpan must have been standing sentry, because as soon my mother rang the bell, the door flew open.

"Come in! Come in!" she welcomed me and my mother. "Your boy has grown into a fine young man!"

"We thank God for little mercies," my mother responded.

"Yes, we should thank the good Lord," Mrs Akpan said. "What drink would you like? I have soft drinks and malt drinks. I am afraid I don't have any beer."

"Blood of Jesus!" my mother exclaimed. "My son does not drink beer."

Mrs Akpan smiled. "You never know with these young men." Then she called out to her daughter to bring some malt drinks.

"So how is Lagos?" she asked me.

I told her about the changes that were taking place in the city: the new lanes created for government-owned buses, the master plan for New Lagos, the furore over the new toll gates. I was still speaking when Idara, the woman's daughter, brought the drinks. My eyes caught the sure steps, the ankara dress and then her face. My mother was right, she was a beauty to behold.

"Should I open the drink for you?" she asked me as she bent over the side stool.

"Please open the drink for him," her mother said before I could respond.

Idara's hands were shaking as she poured the drink into the glass. I watched her and when the glass was half-filled, I told her that it was enough.

"You know my daughter, don't you?" Mrs Akpan asked my mother.

"Of course, I do," she responded. "But I am not sure my son has met her before."

Mrs Akpan performed a quick introduction. She told me that Idara had studied Theatre Arts, but now she worked for herself as a photographer.

"Idara, why don't you show Ifiok some of your photos?" she asked. "I am sure he would like to see the people you have photographed."

Our mothers suddenly rose up from their seats. "Come and show me that wrapper that you were talking about," my mother told her friend. There was no wrapper. They wanted to make sure we would have time alone.

When Idara brought her album, I was momentarily speechless. It was the sort of pictures that I had seen in *National Geographic*, like the image of Ibok taken atop a hill, showing the city displaying its flora of remarkable diversity and richness. Those images of pristine and unspoiled vegetation were of the original Niger Delta.

"I would never have thought there would be a female photographer in Ibok," I said. "You are amazing. What made you go into photography?"

Idara laughed. "It was a hobby at first. I had an old camera that I played around with. My mother used to tease me then. Neighbours liked it when I photographed their children. So when I graduated and there was no job, I decided to go into full-time photography."

"This is an award-winning photograph," I pointed to a picture of a frog in motion. "Have you ever considered entering for a photography award?"

Idara smiled. "So you really think my work deserves an award? That's so sweet."

She gave me a look that made my legs tremble. Her eyes shone. Her smile flickered on and off as I commented on how creativity should be encouraged in Ibok.

We were both laughing when my mother came in. "I can see you two are enjoying each other's company," she said warmly.

The laughter died in my throat. Oh the foolishness! Had I not protested when my mother had first brought the matter up?

"We will visit again," my mother assured Mrs Akpan, as we were leaving.

"I look forward to your return," her friend replied confidently.

In the car, my mother sang praises and talked about God's divine plan for His children.

I tried to convince myself that it was Idara's creativity that drew me to her. She was not like Yetunde at all. Idara was shorter, though more beautiful. But it was not her beauty or her body that hooked me. When I had asked her for her number, I told her that I wanted to continue our conversation about photography.

Chapter 21

I reported early at St Mary's College, the training venue for the ex-militants to observe an orientation programme that the coordinators of the programme had arranged for the tutors. The principal of the school welcomed the mentors to his office enthusiastically. "I am proud that the training is taking place here. I am very happy to see peace return to the region. If you need anything, please don't hesitate to ask me."

I introduced myself and my assignment to the four tutors, all practising film makers: Michael would teach directing; Florence, the only lady, would teach production; Nnamso was assigned to teach directing; and Eskor would handle cinematography and editing. Everybody was smiling. Everybody was patting one another on the back. I enjoyed the positive mood.

"This is serious work you have signed up for," the coordinator told the tutors. "You haven't come here to play. You have come here to add value to the lives of these young people."

The coordinator was very experienced according to my research on the internet. He had worked with former child soldiers in Sierra Leone and Liberia.

"I know that most of you don't have any teaching experience," the coordinator said. "That is why we organised this orientation course for you. Some of you are from this region, so you understand the frustrations and the challenges facing young people here. From my experience, when people think of child soldiers, they think of people who are terribly damaged for life. But I've seen the opposite. I have seen stories of resilience, of acceptance, of love in families."

The coordinator distributed a timetable and a course guide that contained all the information about the film course. I leafed through the pages of the booklet and was impressed with how the content overview and course aims were made clear on one page. The annotated reading list also fitted on one page.

"Most course syllabuses are simply unrealistic," the coordinator said. "They are too wide, too detailed and over-ambitious in terms of the level of understanding which students are required to achieve in the time available, so I have kept this training programme very simple."

But the booklet didn't look simple to me. There were a lot of articles on teaching that the tutors were required to read, ranging from beginning to teach to dealing with difficult students.

Michael turned to me when the coordinator was gone. "So you are a radio journalist. I hope your documentary will be objective."

"Yes, it will be," I replied.

"I have done this sort of work before," Nnamso said to Michael. "So I will tell you this: don't kill yourself over it. You are here to teach people who frankly have no hope. No amount of teaching can save them. They are doomed. You have been paid to do a job here. Do it and go. Don't get attached to it. Believe me, it's not worth it."

His words pained me, but what troubled me most was that the other tutors agreed with Nnamso. I wondered what had happened to the ideals of teaching, the joy that came with sharing knowledge. Why had the tutors signed up for the programme if they didn't believe that it could save any of the students?

"My father was a teacher," Nnamso said. "He was so poorly paid he couldn't fulfil all his basic needs. People used to say that a teacher's reward was in Heaven. Can you imagine that? My father died poor. I don't think he is in Heaven. I like teaching, but I like money more. I want my reward here on earth. I will not make the mistake my dad made. Let's put it this way: if they hadn't paid me well, I would not be here to teach."

"So what is wrong about getting married to a woman chosen by your mother?" my cousin Ubong asked me later, when I told him about Idara. "The thing that matters is whether she is a good girl."

We were having a drink at a bar called Gentlemen's Place, Ubong's favourite relaxation spot. It was a membership only bar: fully air-conditioned with giant TV screens. Ubong had asked Funke Adeleke, the lady from the plane, to meet him there.

"Accept Idara," Ubong told me, as he gulped beer. "It is a good thing to marry a woman that your family approves of. My wife was chosen by my auntie, which is why no matter how much I cheat, she will be waiting for me. When we have a quarrel, I don't worry too much, because our families iron out issues neatly."

The soft drink trickled down my throat. I couldn't drink beer like my cousin, as my mother would have started a long sermon about alcohol and godliness.

"Think carefully," Ubong said. "You need peace in your home. Marriage can be a tough one, believe me."

Funke Adeleke arrived at the bar carrying a small Italian fashion bag and Ubong rushed to receive her at the door. Her eyes lit up when she saw me. We hugged and then she asked, "Ifiok, why didn't you tell me you had such a cute cousin?"

"I bet he wanted you for himself," Ubong responded.

The lady smiled. "Is that true?"

"It doesn't matter if it is true," Ubong said. "I have you now and that's settled."

"Ibok is a really nice town," Funke said.

Ubong beamed with the civic pride of a politician. "Have you seen our new fountain? It's the best in the Niger Delta. Thank God the militants did not blow that up."

He ordered pepper soup with roast snail. Ubong's appetite could have earned him an award. The man ordered five plates for himself. "Some have food but cannot eat," he said when he saw my expression. "Some can eat, but have no food. I have food and I can eat, so why can't I eat well?"

When Ubong brought up the topic of building a branch of their bank in Ibok, Funke didn't seem enthusiastic. "Do you think that would make good business sense?" she asked.

Ubong laughed. "Do you know where you are? This is Ibok! The land of milk and honey. We have so much money here we don't know what to do with it. Do you know how much allocation I get every month from the federal government?"

The lady shook her head and I hoped that Ubong would not start boasting, that the beer wouldn't loosen his tongue.

"There's money in this town!" he claimed. "Too much money! If you bring your bank here, I will give you land to build on for free. Now, how about that?"

"Can we discuss this in private?" Funke asked.

Ubong sprang up. "Why not? I like private talks. I even have a private room here in this motel. So we can go there to discuss the matter in more depth."

I gazed after them as they disappeared down the corridor. Suddenly, a fat woman ran past me straight to the table on the other side of the bar.

"I have caught you today," the woman screamed. "You good-for-nothing husband snatcher. It is me and you today!"

I twisted round to get a better view. The woman at the table, who was a lot slimmer, stood up but her companion did not move. In fact, he carried on drinking his beer as if nothing at all had happened.

"Who is a husband snatcher?" the slim lady asked. "There must be something wrong with your head!"

The fat woman laughed in her face. "I will show you that something is wrong with my head. I will show you madness!"

The women slapped and grabbed at each other and the fat woman managed to grasp the slim one by the neck.

"Pull her hair!" yelled the man who had been sipping beer. "Can't a man have some peace? Since the day I married you, it's been fight after fight. Pull her hair!" The slim lady pulled so hard that the man's wife loosened her grip on the lady's throat and fell down. As she struggled to get up, her dress rode up her thighs to show her flesh. I looked away.

"Stop this nonsense!" commanded the owner of the bar, striding into the bar. She was over six feet tall with arms like yam tubers. She held both troublesome women by their clothes and dragged them out. Without a word to the man who had caused the fight, the bar owner returned to her office.

I told Ubong about the fight when he emerged from his private room.

"Oh really," Ubong responded with little interest. "I have seen enough fights to last me a lifetime."

As he accompanied Funke out of the bar, I noticed that

Ubong gave her a gift.

"I really enjoyed your company, Funke. I will see you later, so we can talk about the contract."

Ubong continued drinking, but I'd had enough, so I left the Gentleman's Place.

At home, I lay in bed listening to the voice of my mother calling upon the God of Abraham to deliver Nigeria from consuming fire. Then I started to think about Yetunde. Was she still in Nigeria? She had changed her number, so I couldn't reach her. When my phone rang, I jumped up to answer it, but it was only Boniface who called to enquire whether I had found myself a woman.

Chapter 22

My father asked me to take some professional debt collectors to recover his rent from a man called Charles, one of the tenants in Father's Lodge. When I protested, he told me, "You are my only child. You need to learn these things now. You have to see how this is done. One day, I will be gone and you will have to deal with these people all alone. Charles has not paid his rent for a while and he won't move out of the house. I need professional debt collectors to help me out here. These guys have been to the house before. They know the drill, so don't worry about anything. Just supervise the process. Don't let things get too nasty."

I sighed. Another uncomfortable rite of passage. The problem was that the so-called debt collectors were thugs who hung around at the motor park. Things could easily get nasty.

"Dad is not in!" Charles' five-year-old son announced sweetly, on seeing us.

"Did we ask you," Paulo, the broad-shouldered thug snapped, "you little rascal? Do you know how much your father owes?"

"Your father can run," Chris, the even more broad-shouldered thug growled at the boy. "Remember, what goes up must come down. We will be here, waiting."

We did not wait long. Charles' Kawasaki announced his

arrival. In the entire community, he was the only man who drove that brand of motorcycle. It was a noisy thing, and most people covered their ears when his machine roared past. Paulo remained still until the man had parked the motorcycle, then he rushed at him. Immediately, Charles slipped and hit his head on an electricity pole.

"What is the meaning of this?" he asked.

"What is the meaning of not paying your rent?" Paulo mimicked. "I need the money! Now!"

Charles licked his lips. "Please, sir," he begged. "I will pay you once my salary has been paid. You know my boss kept the money for our salaries in a bank that has failed. We have not been paid since last year. I swear..."

"I am tired of your stories," Chris pushed in and grabbed Charles' trousers. "I sent you a message that we were coming to collect the rent. I need it now!"

I heard that Charles was the chief typist in the Ministry of Culture, but most people knew that he had an old typewriter in the house that he used for private practice. He typed everything from wills to tenancy agreements. In recent years, higher education students came to rely on him for the last minute typing of their term papers. Even the Reverend Sam, vicar of St. Joseph's Church, trusted Charles to type the regular reports that he sent to the church office in England.

"Why are you pulling my trousers?" Charles screamed. "Do you want to naked me?"

Paulo chuckled. "What if we naked you, eh? What is inside those trousers that I have never seen? Maybe I should see how big you are, eh?" Charles was trying to scrabble back as Paulo and Chris worked at collecting his trousers.

My eyes rested on the man's bag, a leather bag, the type not sold in shops. It was the type they gave out at big weddings as souvenirs. Charles' bag bore the picture of the newlyweds and the words "To God Be the Glory." It was unlikely that Charles knew the couple. These bags were often passed on, from hand to hand, from family to friend. The thugs noticed what I was looking at.

Paulo and Chris let go of Charles suddenly and again, Charles lost his balance, this time landing his buttocks in a pool of urine. Chris grabbed the bag.

"Let go of my bag!" the man screamed.

Paulo spat. "Pay us the rent, then we will return your bag."

"There are confidential documents in that bag," the man said. "Please don't get me in trouble. I beg you in God's name. This is my life."

When Charles saw that the debt collectors were not going to relent, he said, "All right, give me a few minutes to go inside the house. I will give you the rent."

We waited. A few minutes later, he emerged with the money and the thugs returned his bag. When I got home, my father congratulated me. "You have done well," he said.

But I didn't want to live that life. My father's businesses were of no interest to me at all. I couldn't wait to be through with the documentary so I could run back to Lagos.

Chapter 23

Nsima was the first student to arrive for the film class for ex-militants. He didn't fit my idea of a militant at all. He had no blood-shot eyes, nor was his voice husky. He was a lanky boy with a tiny voice and, most unlikely of all, he dressed smartly with a clean white shirt tucked neatly into green trousers.

"You are quite early," I told him. "Classes will not start for another hour."

Nsima smiled. He was happy to wait, he said. In the middle of the night, his mother had begged him to stop pacing and sleep. He asked me how could he sleep when he had been given a second chance. He was starting his life all over again. He was going to be a new man. He, an ex-militant, a university dropout, a failed footballer, was being reborn. He was too excited to sleep.

He told me that he had once thought of himself as a good football player. His bedroom wall was decorated with posters of Beckham, Rooney, Okocha, Kanu and Obafemi; international footballers whom he adored. His transistor radio was permanently tuned to a sport station.

I had read about the successes of Nigerian footballers in Europe. With the money he received playing for a club in England, Okocha had built a skyscraper in Aba. There was chatter at Radio Sunrise that another Nigerian footballer, Kanu Nwankwo, had twenty houses in Lagos. Twenty houses!

My heart had somersaulted upon hearing the news.

Nsima told me he used to play for Ibok United, a local football club, a long time ago. This community club was sponsored by Chief Okokon, a former employee of Southern Oil, who said that this was his way of giving something back to the community.

Nsima gasped when he heard that I did not support any English team. He wondered what sort of Nigerian did not support Arsenal, Manchester United or Aston Villa.

"Good luck to those of you who adorn your rooms with football paraphernalia," I said. "But remember there's more to life than football. Not everybody can be a footballer or a fan."

Nsima assured me firmly that football was a powerful way of building communities and creating harmony. I thought him a smart young man, and imagined him on a football pitch, dribbling his way into the hearts of female fans.

"Not everybody in this country has a second chance," Nnamso, the tutor, announced to begin the class. "But you have been given one, so count yourself lucky. Remember this: everybody makes mistakes. I have made many and I regret them, but life must go on. At the end of this training, you will be able to make your own movie."

Nsima grinned as he leaned forward from his bench. I could hardly imagine the dreams running through his head. Nnamso spoke well. He didn't spout long condemnations, nor quotations from the scriptures; just a simple message of hope and redemption. I noted everything.

"I want you to believe in yourself," Nnamso said. "I want you to believe that if you work hard, you will succeed. Some of you dream of a good life. A life of comfort. If you work hard, you will get it. It's that simple."

The tutor then spoke about the film production process and about the resilience of Nigerian filmmakers. He explained some production jargon: cues, signature tunes, montage. I looked around the class. The ex-militants were a mixed bunch. Henry, the boy sitting on the front row, was scribbling furiously in his notepad. He was a local boy whose attempts to sound sophisticated failed, much to the annoyance of Etido, the boy who fancied himself a wordsmith. Affiong was the only female in the class. Despite her beauty, she wore a formidable expression on her face at all times. I knew it was not unusual for women to get involved in the militant movement. Although these women rarely fought, their unthreatening demeanour often meant they could traffic weapons and other equipment without being intercepted.

I took my own notes. The class had begun well.

Chapter 24

My first proper date with Idara took place in a restaurant called Fine Things. Founded by a Lebanese family who had lived in Ibok for decades, the restaurant was located in the heart of town, close to the newly created business district. Its car park could take up to twenty cars. Sometimes, when a grand car pulled up, the aged restaurateurs came out to pay homage to the wealthy patron.

"Sir, what would you like to order?" the waiter asked me.

I had trouble choosing my meal from the menu. Should I eat the hommos special topped with minced goat meat or should I eat the fassoulyeh, marinated beans with diced vegetables? Idara came to my rescue. "I think you should eat the hommos special," she said. "It's nice."

I took her advice. "Do you come here often?"

"Not very often," she said.

She wore a blue skirt that reminded me vividly of a similar outfit that Yetunde owned, but my ex could not have worn it with such a clinging blouse.

"So tell me about your girlfriend," Idara suddenly asked.

"What girlfriend?" I asked.

She smiled. "I know you Lagos bad boys. You come back to the village pretending to be single, pretending to be looking for a wife, when all the time you have someone living with you in Lagos."

"I had a girlfriend until recently, but we parted amicably."

"Really? What happened?"

"She got a job in the US." The whole story would wait for another day. I couldn't bring myself to tell Idara about the unfortunate incident with the intern Sarah. When our orders arrived, I ate like one who hadn't eaten all day.

"Isn't it funny that our mothers should connect us?" Idara asked me at the end of the meal.

It was strange that we should both be enjoying each other's company. We held hands and when our eyes locked, I wanted to kiss her, but common sense prevailed so I told her about the ex-militants and their film class instead. Idara said she wouldn't mind photographing them. Then to my astonishment, she began to pray quietly for me, covering me with the blood of Jesus, asking the angels to protect me from harm.

I was permitted to go to the ex-militant's class with my voice recorder the next day. I was looking forward to recording activities rather than speeches.

"You need to learn how to put your viewers' needs first to structure your narrative," Michael, the tutor, said. "Today, I want you to watch a short Nollywood film. We will discuss it afterwards."

I settled back to watch the movie too. It was a simple story about two brothers. The younger one was married but he couldn't procreate. The older brother, who was not married, had developed lung cancer and was expected to die within six months. The desperate younger brother asked the older brother to impregnate his wife so that their family lineage would not be wiped out.

"We will end it there for today," Michael announced suddenly, as he switched off the video.

Henry immediately protested. I smiled. "Sir," the student began in his poor English, "it was not fair. Couldn't we finished the film?"

"What I have done is called suspense," the tutor informed his class. "Suspense is the soul of any movie. If there's no suspense, then there's no movie."

Another student, Etido, said, "Is this a deliberate attempt to obfuscate or envelope our minds?"

The class laughed and challenged him to explain the meaning of his comment, but Etido, nicknamed "the Grammarian", said nothing more.

"So can we guess what might happen next in the film?" Nsima suddenly asked.

All eyes in the class suddenly turned to him. Nsima tried to hide his face with his book. "That's a good question," Michael said warmly. "Shall we guess?"

Henry put up his hand. "If I am the senior brother, I will give the wife a long-lasting and very expensive fucking."

Many people laughed. I did not know if such language was permitted in class, so I felt relieved when I saw the tutor smiling.

"But my people, it's a good thing to ask your brother's help when circumstances like this make an appearance," Henry said. "After all, we say 'be your brother's keeper.'"

Everyone laughed.

Idara, aware that I was a man who loved to look after his stomach, invited me to her house for a homemade dinner. She said she wanted to welcome me back to Ibok properly with a sumptuous meal of afia efere with stockfish and pounded yam. It was an offer too alluring to resist. The sweet aroma hit me even before Idara opened the door and welcomed me with a very wide smile. She wore a tight blouse that accentuated her shape. "Thank you for coming," she said as she led me to the dining area.

"Is your mother home?" The words jumped out of my mouth.

"No," she responded. "She has gone to a meeting of the Ibok Women's Association." She moved into the living room. "Let me tell you about the lady I photographed today."

As she prepared the table, she told me about Mrs Ekanem, the proprietor of Prudent Hair Salon, a recent alumna of the New York International Beauty Academy. Her trip abroad and subsequent overseas studies had been sponsored by Southern Oil, as part of the company's corporate social responsibility. She had gone through a fierce selection process. The judges, a former beauty queen, a professor of dermatology at the University of Calabar, a director from the Ministry of Women's Affairs and a representative from the Niger Delta Congress, had selected her. When Mrs Ekanem returned from the United States, she did so with a false American accent. She started wearing American dresses too, T-shirts bearing the inscription "I love America" and short skirts in the colours of the American flag.

"She insisted on wearing the American outfits for the the photograph," Idara said and I laughed. I could picture the woman in the heat of an Ibok room, posing in a winter coat for the camera. "After I finished," Idara continued, "the lady served Jolt Cola, Mountain Dew and Root Beer, drinks she insisted she'd bought at an American supermarket."

Idara smiled when I said I could not wait to taste her cooking. Afia efere was also known as white soup, although the soup was anything but white. Sometimes, to thicken it, pounded yam was moulded into small rounds and dropped into the soup. I washed my hands and launched my assault on the food.

"A great dish," I said, as I wiped oil from my mouth. "I miss such delicacies in Lagos."

"I didn't put too much pepper in the soup," Idara said. "I didn't know if you liked pepper."

"No, I don't. Food that contains too much pepper does not suit my stomach."

Idara wanted me to talk about my documentary, but for a while I only spoke about the soup. I wanted to know how she had prepared it, if she had used a recipe, something I could take back to Lagos with me.

"If you are nice to me, I could teach you," she told me.

"I would like that."

"Of course, my darling."

My heart skipped. She had called me her darling. I wanted to dance. I helped her clear the dishes. In the tiny kitchen, when she hugged me, when her lips grazed my cheek, my body came alive, but I held myself back. It had to be different with Idara. It was not necessary for us to go all the way until we were sure we were going somewhere.

"Where have you been?" my mother asked me when I got home. "I have been trying to reach you."

It was then that I realised that my phone had been mistakenly switched off. "I was with Idara. She invited me over for a meal."

My mother's face softened into a smile. "That is very good. What did she offer you? Did you enjoy it? She's a very good cook, isn't she?"

For several minutes my mother extolled the virtues of Idara in quite a lecture. She said that a rich politician had wanted to marry her a year ago. I didn't ask questions when she said Idara turned down the marriage offer. "She's a very good lady," my mother said. "Take it from me."

That evening, I called Boniface to find out what was going on in Radio Sunrise.

"It's a bit dull here," he replied. "No new girl to tickle my fancy. How about you? How are you coping with the documentary?"

"The documentary is going on well," I said, but I didn't tell him about Idara.

After the call, I began to think more about my photographer friend. I didn't know much about jewellery but I did know that the pieces she wore were expensive. Her car was expensive too. Was she making a fortune taking people's photos? These thoughts swam in my head before sleep drowned me.

Chapter 25

"Somebody help me! Somebody please help!" a voice rang out outside the house. I leapt up from my bed.

There was only one "screaming machine" in the neighbourhood. Agnes screamed whenever her drunken husband turned her into a punching bag and she screamed in the mornings, when she went about selling her fresh bread.

It was six thirty in the morning and that was not Agnes' scream I could hear. What could be wrong? My journalistic instincts were roused. I grabbed my voice recorder and ran out to find that a food canteen was burning.

"My mistress is inside," screamed the cook who had woken me and many of the neighbours. "Please, don't let her burn to death!"

I did not join the good Samaritans who were helping to quench the inferno with makeshift fire fighting equipment. I stood far away from the kiosk, but close enough to record the sounds. Someone arrived with fresh palm leaves and another came with a bucketful of holy water. "This has been blessed by Bishop David," the woman announced very loudly, but her holy water could not put out the fire. The fire service crew arrived soon after without fire fighting equipment.

"Is it your saliva that you will use to put out this fire?" someone asked their supervisor.

The man, probably used to such encounters, retorted, "The

government did not make an allocation for us this year. We are surviving on donations from the public."

I turned to look at the speaker. His face was strained, with small dark eyes. There was a large hole in his uniform. He bore a striking resemblance to the traffic warden I had seen at the Aba Road roundabout.

"So why are you here?" an old man asked the fire chief. "You have no equipment to put out this fire?"

"Well," the chief replied. "I came to observe so that I can write a report."

"God punish you!" someone cried out.

"May your house burn to ashes!" another proclaimed.

It was Udot who cast the first stone; Udot whose middle name was Troublemaker. His father was a retired soldier, who had returned from a peacekeeping mission in Rwanda a very different person. People gossiped that there was an illness in the head that ran in their family.

"Are you out of your minds?" one of the officers shrieked. "How dare you hit a uniformed man? You will pay dearly for this. You will…"

But the man and his crew took to their heels when Udot became bolder and smashed a bottle—a beer bottle, I noted. The man from Nigerian Breweries who supplied shopkeepers with beer always shouted out, "Liquid contents only!" since the bottles themselves belonged to the breweries.

Chief Ekpo, the proprietor of Evergreen Waters opened the door to his water factory. He didn't mind, he said, that all the water in his factory be used to put out the raging fire.

"Don't just stand there!" Chief Ekpo barked at someone. "Do something. Get a bucket, a pot, anything. Let's put out this fire!"

People tried their best to put out the fire. When the

restaurateur was rescued from the inferno, she wasn't badly burnt. I was relieved that someone volunteered to take her to the hospital. We heard that the cause of the fire was a kerosene explosion in the stove. The restaurateur had bought adulterated kerosene from one of the shady filling stations in Ibok.

I needed to decide if it was necessary to include the scene in my documentary. I paused my recording and went back to the house. My mother was already preparing breakfast. I had a quick meal, rushed a bath and dashed out to the ex-militant's class.

"In your movie," Nnamso told his class, "your characters must be believable. When you write your dialogue, read it out to yourself. If it doesn't sound right, then go back and work on it."

I switched on my voice recorder. I wasn't really interested in the tutor's words, to be honest, but he wanted to feature in the documentary.

Nnamso continued, "There was a time that female characters in most films were portrayed as weak wives, mothers or daughters desperately in need of the male hero's affection and protection. Times have changed, we now have movies showing women as heroines."

"But what about actors who can only play a particular role?" Nsima asked. He had seen it several times, he said. Mama G, for instance always played the role of a wicked mother or mother-in-law. She was never the nice lady.

"I believe an actor must be versatile," the tutor responded. "He or she must be able to play any role."

"That one cannot be true," Henry said. "There are some people born only to play a certain role. That is their lifestyle. Can you imagine Osuofia playing a serious role?"

Osuofia, the king of Nigerian comedy, had appeared in over 200 movies, but always played comical roles. Sometimes, he acted the local drunk; at other times, he was just an old fool.

"Tell me," Henry continued, "do you think Osuofia can act the role of a managing director? Do you think he can be a doctor?"

I myself could not imagine Osuofia playing the role of an astute business man. Who would take him seriously?

"I think the problem is that he would not be taken seriously even if he acted a serious role really well," Affiong said.

"That's stereotyping then," the tutor said. "It's a common occurrence in movie industries around the world. In Hollywood, the stereotypical view is that black people are drug dealers and gangsters. They are rarely shown as professionals."

"Me, I wouldn't enjoy a film where Osuofia is playing a doctor or engineer," Henry said. "In fact, I wouldn't watch the film at all. Simple."

"I feel even more nauseated and vexed that you should say this," Etido said. "You shouldn't let such morphemes escape your vocal cavity."

"The Grammarian!" The class roared with laughter. "Etido, the Grammarian!"

"Take it upon yourself to challenge the stereotypes," Nnamso instructed his students. "Show the rest of Nigeria that you are more than mindless kidnappers and thugs, that you are productive members of society. Take it upon yourself to write a movie or produce one with Osuofia playing a serious role."

"I don't think people will watching it," Henry argued. "People are so used to be see him in particular way. So the film will be a fat flop."

The tutor smiled. "The truth is, if your story is good then you have nothing to worry about. I agree that Osuofia has only played comical roles. So if you must cast him in a more serious role, make it believable. Don't let your film become formulaic and straitjacketed."

I jotted "formulaic" down in my notebook. It was a good word to use in my documentary.

Chapter 26

"Hey, watch where you are going!" I shouted at a young boy who had just cycled into the fence of the roofless building housing the Day of Joy Tutorial Centre. The boy fell, but got up immediately and climbed back on his bike.

"Boys will be boys!" he announced as he cycled away.

Nostalgia overwhelmed me as I remembered taking delight in riding my uncle's old Raleigh bicycle in our tiny compound. As a young boy, my parents never allowed me to cycle along the main road.

When I arrived at the Cornel Cool Corner, Idara was just driving in. "I hope you'll like this restaurant," she said as we were seated.

We had agreed to lunch together whenever we could. They only sold local delicacies at Cornel Cool Corner: eba, coconut rice, afang. The menu was on the table, but one of the waiters came and asked if we would like a "404." In Ibok, a dog was called "404" after the Peugeot pick-up van, in recognition of a dog's running ability. My people believed in the efficacy of charms. They believed that eating dog meat could give one a special protection against all sorts of ailments. Like Cornel Cool Corner, Loco, an open-air joint next to a small river on the outskirts of Ibok also sold dog meat, but that restaurant was notorious for its gamblers and other undesirable elements.

I gave the dog meat a pass and settled for spicy goat head.

When the food arrived, the meat was soft.

"Really nice," I said. "These guys are good."

Idara agreed. "It's always good to have a nice restaurant where you can run to if you are bored with your own cooking. The owner is a very nice man. And he makes lots of money from this place. He's been able to send three of his children abroad to study."

During the meal, so many questions about Idara raced through my mind. Why was a pretty woman like her still single? Surely, apart from the one my mother told me about, she must have received many marriage proposals? What did she really want? Where was she getting the money for all the expensive things she wore?

"Why are you looking at me like that?" she asked me.

"You are very beautiful," I said. "I am surprised no man has whisked you away before."

Her face broke into dimples. Her eyes were bright and deep. I wanted to touch her cheeks. I wanted to touch her hair.

"Maybe I have been waiting for you," she said. "You are a breath of fresh air. You are pure, nothing at all like the men in Ibok."

Oh, music to my ears! The words caressed me and made me close my eyes for a brief moment. When I opened them, Idara was leaning forward. "So tell me about your ex-girlfriend in Lagos," she said. "The one you said went abroad."

I almost choked. Any thought of Yetunde made my blood hot. It was better for me to keep my mouth shut.

"You still like her, don't you?" Idara pressed.

I shook my head. "Its over. It didn't work. It could not have worked even if she was still in the country. She's Yoruba."

It was safer to play the ethnicity card. I was Ibibio; Yetunde was Yoruba: two very different ethnic groups, so there would have been difficulty along the way with our families, I told Idara.

Idara bought the story. "So you wanted to bring a Yoruba woman to show your mother? You are a bold man o!"

"That's why I said it was not working," I responded. "My father would have killed me, I swear."

"But if she was from Ibok, you would have married her, right?"

"I don't know. She's so different from you."

"How?"

"I can't explain."

The owner of the restaurant suddenly walked in and Idara leapt up to greet him. "Meet my friend, Ifiok," she introduced me. "He is a journalist."

His T-shirt barely covered his protruding stomach. The man gave me a wide smile and a gripping handshake. "Ah, a journalist! Welcome home. Perhaps, you could help advertise my restaurant? I need more people to know about our excellent food. I need more customers."

"Ah, Mr Ekanem," Idara said. "You like money o!"

The man smiled. "Yes, I do. I need money to be able to maintain my lifestyle."

Idara drove me home afterwards. In bed, I lay awake thinking about her. Beautiful Idara. Adorable Idara. But what about her expensive lifestyle? My affection for her could not be debated, but I had an unsettling feeling about her.

My phone rang. It was my cousin, Ubong. "Ifiok, where are you?" he asked.

"I am home."

"What are you doing at home? You should be having fun. I am at the Gentleman's Place. Funke Adeleke just left here. Oh my goodness, that lady is sweet. Take it from me. Her honey pot is the best I have tasted in a while. I have been with many women, but she stands out. It was a marathon. I was at it for two hours. Non-stop. She has agreed to bring her bank here. Isn't that great news? We sealed the deal in the bedroom. I can't wait! We have already discussed..."

Before Ubong finished speaking, I fell asleep.

Ubong was a guest speaker at the ex-militants' training course the next day. He came with five official cars and ten armed body guards. He wore a white suit that made me think of a popular charismatic preacher in Lagos.

"I am very delighted to be here," Ubong told the students. "I am proud of you. I am proud that so many of you have said no to violence. It is a good thing that you have allowed peace to prevail in the community. When there's peace, communities thrive."

Someone's mobile phone played a popular ring tone; a song about money and sex. Ubong waited for the phone to stop ringing before he continued.

"I know that the government has failed young people in the community," he said. "I know that despite many years of oil and gas, the majority of our people living in the Niger Delta remain poor. I was frustrated too, which is why I went to politics. I was tired of simply watching and doing nothing. I am happy and proud that you have heeded this new government's call for amnesty. I assure you that you have made the right choice."

The ex-militants applauded. I clapped too. My cousin had transformed himself into a great public speaker. Ubong must have rehearsed his speech many times, I thought. His delivery was almost flawless.

"This is a new government," Ubong reminded the people.

"This is a new government that listens and acts. Be assured that we know about your frustrations. Be assured that we are making progress towards addressing these issues. We know that electricity is key to development, and that's why the government is investing more funds in power generation. In two years, the people of this community will be enjoying an uninterrupted power supply."

The cheer was resounding. In fact, a lot of people clapped for so long that my cousin had to raise his hands to indicate they should stop.

"Brothers, believe me, I understand what it means to be hungry, what it means to be angry," Ubong continued. "I understand because I have been there. But I am happy that you are here now. We have ambitious plans for you, now that you seek peace. We can now reason together. We can now decide what skills you have, what jobs you can do. You will not regret surrendering your weapons."

It was difficult for people to doubt Ubong's words. He was part of the community. He had been on the bottom rung of the ladder himself. He knew all about poverty. After his talk, he shook hands and even hugged some of the ex-militants. He held Affiong, the only girl in the class, a bit longer than the others. When he let go of her hands, he whispered something to her.

"What did you tell her?" I asked him.

Ubong laughed. "What is it to you? Anyway, I told her that she's very pretty and I would be honoured to take her out."

While filling my tank at a petrol station on my way back from the training course, someone appeared and asked me if I wanted my windscreen washed as a free service.

In Ibok, it was difficult to say no to anything free. Men in nice suits have fought over free plates of rice at weddings and funerals. I stepped out of the car and walked up to a comfy chair outside the kiosk. A young lady in a blue trouser suit introduced herself as the manager of the station. She shook my hand.

"Nice to meet you," she said. She was probably in her early twenties. It was very unusual to have young women as managers of service stations. It was even more unusual to see such managers dressed in suits. I took out my voice recorder. She didn't have a problem being interviewed.

"I am a trailblazer," she said. "They say what a man can do, a woman can do better. I am proof of this."

She had studied Business Administration at the University of Uyo. Like most fresh graduates, she longed to work in a bank, where the salary was reasonable and she could wear trouser suits. But after writing several aptitude tests, after she was tossed here and there like a coin, it dawned on her that nepotism was an obstacle to her employment. She then joined her father to run the service station.

"My father had wanted to close down the station because it wasn't making much money," she revealed. "Some people had said that his business was destroyed by witches and wizards, but I asked him to give me a chance to run the it. I introduced new services to the station and new ways of running the business. I got rid of grumbling workers who never had anything good to say. I also fired those who refused to accept change."

It worked, she said. It was like being reborn. Motorists who came were surprised at the attention they received from the workers and loved it. Word went round and more motorists arrived.

"The business picked up considerably," the manager said. "It's amazing what a simple thing like washing a windscreen could do. My dad was very pleased. I was very pleased. Perhaps, if I had been working at the bank, I wouldn't be this pleased."

"Do you secretly thank God that you did not get the job then?" I asked.

The lady smiled. "Sometimes."

It was certainly one of the most refreshing stories I had heard from Ibok in recent times. And it would make a good addition to my documentary. I encouraged her to keep up her good work as I drove off.

Chapter 27

The Ibok branch of the Artisan Fishermen Association of Nigeria demanded 24 million naira in compensation for damages caused by the oil spill at Obot Ima oil fields. Everyone took the basic points of the news item and added several twists to it to make it their own. My father's guests gathered in the sitting room to debate the issue. I listened from my bedroom. A guest, who claimed to have studied a module on biodiversity, pointed out to the others that the spill had polluted the waters and scared the fish deeper into the Atlantic Ocean.

"And what will the money do?" my father asked. "Will it bring back the fish?"

"The compensation would cover damages and losses incurred by fishermen," someone quickly responded. "You know fish cannot breed at the creeks during the rainy season due to the effects of the oil spill: the result is a scarcity of fish."

"I will tell you exactly what was in the letter," another said. "I saw the letter myself. The same copy that was sent to the governor and the president of Nigeria. I memorised the contents. The letter read: 'The incessant oil spills from the facilities of Erand Oil in Ibok threatens our means of livelihood. The waters where they operate is equally our farm and each time there is a spill, we are thrown out of business for several months.'"

I wished I knew about biodiversity or the breeding patterns

of sea creatures, so I could go to the living room and contribute to the debate.

"You are your father's true son," my father said later when his guests were gone. "You came to Ibok to see and conquer. And you have conquered, haven't you? You came to do a documentary, but you have also learnt a few things about looking after the family. You can handle my tenants and, most importantly, you have found a wife. I am a happy man."

My mother was in the kitchen, preparing a meal. I could smell the spices. I could hear her giving orders to the housegirl to bring her some water, to stir the pot. Soon, she would join Dad and me on the veranda.

"Have some more wine," my father said. "You remind me so much of my youth. When I was your age, I wore your type of beard. Unfortunately, there's no photo to prove that. I lost the pictures during the war."

I sipped the drink. As far I was concerned, it was fruit juice. It shouldn't be called wine. It sounded deceitful.

"Idara is a very good lady," my father continued. "She's from a good home too. That is all you need to make your marriage great. Believe me, you don't want stress in your marriage. A bad marriage is like hell fire."

For the eleventh time that day, my father brought up the discussion on marriage. But I lacked the courage to ask him to stop.

"Your mother is a very strong woman," my father said. "I wouldn't have lived this long without her."

As if on cue, my mother came out and announced that food would be ready soon. When she went back to the kitchen, my father continued to talk about marriage.

"I think we should formally declare our intention to the Akpans," he said. "You will be going back to Lagos soon and it would be good to do something significant before you leave."

The journey towards getting married in Ibok was not for the fainthearted. After a series of meetings, the bride's family had to agree on a list. Often, there was a symbolic price to be paid for the bride, in addition to other items like kola nuts, goats, chickens and palm wine. It always took more than one evening before the final price of the bride was settled.

"Daddy, I have only known Idara for about two weeks," I pointed out.

My father laughed. "It doesn't matter. I know you like her. I see the way you glow when her name is mentioned. You two were made for each other. I know that for sure."

"I think we should give it some more time," I said.

"I am not saying you must marry her today," my father said. "What I am saying is that we should start the process now. Don't the English people say that we should make hay while the sun shines?"

He was asking me to make a serious commitment, I knew that. Once the process had started, it would be difficult to turn back. My father knew that too. "Please, Daddy, let me go back to Lagos and think about it," I said.

"What do you want to think about? You know you like her. So what's the problem?"

The words I wanted to say, the fears of getting married, my concern about Idara's finery formed, ready to be spoken. I was sure they were going to tumble out of my mouth, but they dissolved inside my throat.

"I understand how you feel," my father looked at me shrewdly. "I felt the same way too when I met your mother. You will get used to it."

That night, sleep eluded me. There was a prayer meeting taking place in a nearby house. Their loud singing and crying added to my discomfort. Sleep only came to me towards dawn. Three hours later, I woke up with a start. My left eye was twitching. I wasn't at all superstitious, but it wasn't a good sign for a man to wake up with his left eye twitching so much. But I refused to spend time worrying about it.

When I arrived in class later that day, I knew immediately something was wrong. The course coordinator's voice was low when he announced, "I have sad news for you today. I actually only heard it this morning. The funding for this media programme has been cut. This class is the best the government can do for you. There will be no funds for you to produce your own films. The local government will not be able to…"

"Please tell us you are lying," Nsima interrupted heatedly. "Tell us this is fiction. Tell us you are acting out a script. Tell us it is not real."

Silence filled the classroom. The students fixed their eyes on the coordinator. My heart was sprinting and I was finding it difficult to accept the news. It must have been impossible for the students.

The coordinator sighed heavily and confirmed that the funding had been cut. After the film training class, the ex-militants would receive no more help. I hadn't seen it coming. What about the promise of making the ex-militants filmmakers?

"The politicians lied to us," Nsima said to me. "They said we were going to be supported, that we would be given a means of livelihood. We surrendered our weapons and this is what we get?"

"I think it can be sorted out, I am sure," I quickly said. "I am sure there's been a mistake."

Henry stood up and started shouting, "This is fraud! This is a big trickery. We were tricked! They tell us to surrender our weapons. They tell us we will be looked after. They tell us our lives will be better. Is this their idea of better?"

The coordinator tried to calm them down. "I promise you I will talk to a few people I know in government. You still have a few more days before your course finishes. Anything can still happen. Let us not lose hope."

I would also lose my documentary. The fight was mine as well.

I plodded past Pandy Towers, the most modern building on Miles Road. Rumour had it that the house belonged to a retired military governor.

"This way," the security officer at the desk directed me when I arrived at Ubong's office. "My oga has been expecting you."

Ubong opened the tiny refrigerator by his desk. All kinds of chilled treats were in there: fruit juices, ice creams and soft drinks. I was very privileged. How many people in the city could get through to the vice-chairman of the council? Even to see an ordinary secretary, many people were usually asked for a mobilisation fee at the reception.

"You are not looking bad," Ubong commented. "That means you are enjoying your time here."

I frowned. "I look good? After you cut funding for the amnesty programme?"

"I am not the person who cut the funding," Ubong snapped. "The orders came from above. I didn't even control the funding in the first place."

"This is not fair," I told my cousin. "Why do this to these young people who have chosen to forsake violence? Why dangle the funding in front of them and then take it away? They have kept their part of the agreement."

"I am not the government!" Ubong complained. "I am not the one in charge of funding for the ex-militants. You

166

know that!"

I didn't know what to believe anymore. Who could have taken the decision to cut funding for such a noble gesture? I told my cousin that the decision of the government was painful to me.

"It hurt me too," Ubong responded. "I had been looking forward to watching movies produced by ex-militants."

"Can't you do something?" I asked. "Can't you persuade the people above you to have a change of heart?"

Ubong sighed. "I have written letters, I swear. I have spoken to a few people. Let's see how it goes."

That evening, my father didn't look up when I shuffled into the sitting room. He did not react when I sat beside him on the white couch. He was engrossed in reading the foreign pages of *The Punch*. I sat quietly, knowing that soon, my father would look up and comment on the news story that had interested him so much.

"This is hilarious," he murmured, without looking up. "So very amusing. Sometimes you wonder if we are living in the same universe."

My father looked up finally and thrust the paper at me, pointing to the story of a man in England who blamed his local council for the breakdown of his marriage after he, his wife and their ten children were forced to live together in a flat with only three bedrooms. The man claimed his dream of living together as one big happy family in their modest home had turned into a nightmare. He and his wife could be stuck with each other in this madhouse indefinitely after the council said it could not accommodate them in separate houses. His only option was to declare himself and his family homeless.

"Funny, isn't it?" my father asked soberly. "These Europeans are fighting over a three-bedroomed flat and we are here fighting over kidnapping and oil wealth."

My mother's voice suddenly floated in the room. She sang of love, of power, of rage. She sang of men who have been drowned in the sea of their ambition, of mothers who have buried their children, of children forced into wars and prostitution. Then she sang of God's love, and of how He will wipe the tears from their eyes.

Chapter 28

It took me two hours and twenty minutes to locate Mr Iwat, Nsima's uncle and a retired permanent secretary. He was an influential man. Three different people had given me three wrong descriptions. Eventually, the old woman who sold fresh fish by the IBB Roundabout told me, without looking up from her basin of fish, that her customer of many years lived three houses away from the Customary Court in a yellow building with blue roof. I could not miss it, she added.

"Who is it?" a voice asked, when I knocked on the door.

"Good day, sir. Please, is Mr Iwat at home?"

There was a shuffling of feet then a loud cough, and then silence. I stepped back when the door swung open. Mr Iwat was a tall man. A large pair of spectacles rested on his nose. He did not look anything like I had imagined. He was clean shaven, with a complete set of white teeth and a face that made one immediately think of a kitten.

"Who are you?" the man asked.

"I am Ifiok, a reporter from Radio Sunrise. I came to interview you for a programme."

Broadcast journalists are taught to feel comfortable with thousands, sometimes millions of people looking at their face or listening to their voice. I had a likeable face. And my voice could melt even the hardest hearts. A smile broke out on Mr Iwat's face and he invited me into his living room. I relaxed.

My charm was at work again.

"I am blessed," Mr Iwat suddenly said. "A journalist from a radio station has come to visit me. I am blessed."

My eyes were drawn to the walls of the man's sitting room, from the china on the bookshelf, to the framed diplomas, to the many black and white photographs of his family.

"The many wonders of the camera," the man whispered, his eyes following mine. "Isn't it amazing that a click of a button can just document your life forever?"

The day my camera was stolen at an event in Lagos, I had felt the strange feeling that grief brings, the long, terrible numbness that made me lose my appetite.

How could I start my discussion with Mr Iwat? What would my former tutor, the enigmatic man who referred to documentaries as the aristocracy of radio, have said? I swallowed. Leaning close, speaking deliberately in carefully chosen words, I slipped in Nsima's name.

"I don't want to hear that name in this house!" Mr Iwat screamed.

The change in him was startling. Mr Iwat put down his glasses and crossed his legs. I held my breath.

"That boy is not my nephew," Mr Iwat broke the silence. "He has never been my nephew. How he got born into this family, I do not know. I don't want to see him until he is cured of witchcraft."

I had known it would be difficult talking about Nsima, but I had prepared. I had promised myself that I would be patient, that I would not hurry the man. My tutor always said, "the broadcast journalist needs to be able to stay calm under pressure."

"We live in an evil world, Ifiok," Mr Iwat continued, "a very evil world. Do you read the Bible?" But before I could say anything, the man continued, "The Bible tells us, you and me, for we wrestle not against flesh and blood, but against principalities, against powers, against the rulers of the darkness of this world, against spiritual wickedness in high places. I have read the verse since my childhood, but it never occurred to me that this verse would manifest itself in my own family."

He paused for a little longer and I worried whether or not the man would resume talking or if I would have to prompt him. When he began talking again, his tone seemed calmer, softer.

"That boy ruined us," Mr Iwat revealed. "He brought shame upon my family. In the beginning, the militants said they were fighting for the good of the land, but they were just criminals. If they were fighting for the good of the land, wouldn't they have used their ransom money to develop the land? No! They are criminals and the government should never have talked about amnesty. The so-called militants should all be in jail!"

"But sir, they have repented."

The man laughed. "You think they have? Do not be deceived. Those boys can never repent. They are evil."

"Sir, the funding for the amnesty programme has been cut," I said. "Can't you influence any important men to make sure that funding continues?"

"It's a good thing the funding was cut," Mr Iwat said. "It was a bloody waste of money and time."

I could not remember how I lost my calm, how I screamed at the man, for not wanting to help the ex-militants. I remembered the man jumping up from his chair, remembered him holding on to my collar and screaming, "What do you know, eh? You know nothing! You think that you can come here and tell me nonsense? You are a goat. You are a fool! Get out of my house. If I see you anywhere around here again, I swear I will break your legs!"

"Your cousin is here," my mother whispered when I climbed out of the car. There was something in her tone, something in the way that she said it that made me shiver.

The smell of eggs, beans and onion hit me when I opened my bedroom door. My cousin's farts, no doubt.

"For God's sake, Ubong, please open the window," I exclaimed.

"Don't open the window!" Ubong responded. His voice quivered. I saw the fear in his face, too.

"What is it?" I asked as I sat down, holding my breath as best I could. I was trying to remember if there was any air freshener in the house.

"They are after me," Ubong cried. "The kidnappers have taken the local government chairman. They came after me, to my house. I escaped, but they are searching for me, I know that. I have to run away, to Lagos maybe. I have arranged for someone to come here to pick me up. Someone I trust."

I didn't know what to say. It seemed that upon learning that the government was not serious about the amnesty programme, some ex-militants had resumed their attacks and kidnappings. They had even threatened to unleash mayhem in Ibok.

"I cannot stay in my house," Ubong said. "I can't stay anywhere in this town. Nowhere is safe. Nowhere at all."

I remembered the security devices surrounding my cousin's house. I remembered his armed guards. It was a shame that they couldn't protect him.

"I am so afraid," Ubong whispered. "I am so very afraid."

The person I saw, the image before me, though vaguely familiar was not my cousin, the politician, the vice-chairman of the local government council. It couldn't be, I thought. He was the Ubong of my childhood, a timid Ubong who didn't dare to raise his hand in class.

Ubong's trusted colleague arrived thirty minutes later in a battered Volkswagen. My mother said a quick prayer for his safety as we watched him being driven out of the compound.

The unfolding hostility in Ibok worried me as I went to visit Idara at her studio. Ubong had infected me with his anxiety, making me too nervous to drive. At the nearby bus stop, there was a long row of motorbike taxis riders. The riders, mostly men, wore yellow vests. The government had made it compulsory for these men to wear uniforms, to separate them from other riders who used motorbikes for nefarious activities.

"I beg you in the name of God," I told an elderly man. "Ride carefully."

I clung to the motorbike to prevent myself from falling. I sat so close to the man that I was able to see a rash on his neck. The motorbike puffed and panted through the metropolis, past the statue of General Bassey, the first indigenous army general, past the ultra-modern banquet hall, past several new generation banks and churches. When we passed the Internal Revenue Office, the cyclist began telling me about the activities of tax officers, how they hid behind banana trees, waiting for unsuspecting motorcyclists to appear.

"They never give receipts, you know," the man announced.

I alighted from the motorcycle and strolled into Idara's studio. There was no one in the reception area so I walked to Idara's office and opened the door. Idara, stark naked, was astride a man I didn't recognise.

I silently reversed.

I walked aimlessly around the town centre. Someone called out, "Good day!" Another said, "Well done." These people knew me or my parents, but I didn't return their greetings. I hardly noticed them. I was struggling with the consequences of knowledge. Would it have been better for me not to know?

Sweat streamed down my face. Still I continued walking. I had no destination. I had read about the healing nature of motion, of the calmness that followed exertion, but it wasn't working.

"How could you, Idara?" I said out loud.

How could she do that to me? She seemed such a decent lady, good, virtuous. All our time together, I had not known her at all, as though I had only been watching the shadow she cast upon the wall.

I walked on, past the polytechnic, where young girls stood in skimpy dresses, waiting and hoping a rich man would pass by and give them a lift. Someone handed me a flyer printed with a message from a church: "For there is nothing covered, that shall not be revealed and hid that shall not be known. Repent now!"

I laughed bitterly. Nothing had been covered up in Idara's studio.

When I eventually got home, I became aware of my headache, but I refused to take medication. I took off my clothes and entered the bathroom. When the warm water hit my skin, I sang praises, songs of liberation, of the power of blood and water. But the blue soap did not lather easily. It did not even smell as nice as Cool, the cheap soap that I bought from the store in my street in Lagos. I raised my hands and scrubbed my armpits as though they were blemished with dirt.

My mother could not understand my changed behaviour. Everything she had planned for had been going well. Why was I no longer interested in Idara? It was the Devil's plan, she said. It was her enemies trying to bring her to shame.

"Ifiok, tell me," she begged, "why have you changed your mind about Idara? What is wrong? I am your mother, talk to me."

Of course I could not talk to her. How could I tell her that their darling Idara was nothing but a "giver"? Oh, that scene in the studio! She had called me to beg for forgiveness or silence; the man had offered her so much money she couldn't refuse. She knew she had lost me, but she didn't want her family to know about her sexual escapades. It was only then that everything fell into place: the expensive jewellery; the expensive car; the expensive clothes. There had to be other men, not just the fellow in the studio. I should have known better. Talk about being an investigative journalist!

"What do you want us to tell her parents?" my mother asked.

"Tell them I am no longer interested in their daughter," I responded.

"God forbid," she muttered.

I needed to get back to Lagos, to get back to Radio Sunrise. I had gone to my hometown as a simple-minded sinner in search of redemption and knowledge. I had become an educated man.

My mother wept. "I can't believe you are going back like this."

My father said, "As you are going back to Lagos, I want you think carefully about your life. You need a wife. We have found you a good woman. Don't let pride get in the way. Think carefully."

Chapter 29

On the plane, the man sitting beside me had extensive tribal marks on his cheeks, like the veins on a leaf. His face was vaguely familiar and I tried desperately to remember where I had seen it. The man blew his nose and then adjusted his seat.

"I do not know what made me do it," the man grumbled.

"What, sir?" I asked.

I couldn't resist staring at the man's face, couldn't resist studying the tribal marks that had scarred his handsome face.

"Are you married?" the man asked me.

"No, sir."

"Ah," the man exclaimed. "They say kids are gifts from God. Well, I do not know anymore. What have I not done for those boys? I took one of them to England to study, so he could avoid the cults in our universities."

The man blew his nose again with a different handkerchief. A disembodied voice came on air to urge passengers to fasten their seatbelts.

"Misfortune has been my lot," the passenger beside me revealed. "You know, there are people in life that misfortune just follows all the way through. Sometimes I wonder if I am one of these people."

I had no idea what the man was talking about, but I was sure that I didn't like the idea of sitting in a plane beside a man with misfortune as his lot. I wished I had my iPod player, so I could put on my earphones and listen to music.

"It is their mother's fault," the man continued, oblivious to my discomfort. "She wouldn't let me rest until I sent the boy to England to study. I thought I did the right thing. You know how much it costs to study in that country? But I paid everything. I paid all his fees in full."

It is my misfortune, I told myself fiercely, *it is my lot to sit beside a loud-mouthed passenger on my return to Lagos. Will I be able to enjoy the flight at all?*

"When we went to the university in Nigeria," the man said, "things were good. We didn't have to bother about cultism, about food, about water scarcity, about kidnappings. All we bothered about was our studies. In a twinkle of an eye, everything changed. The Devil strolled into our campuses and took over the lives of our children. Can you explain to me why a twenty-year-old boy would pull the trigger on his roommate?"

I wanted to ask the man, "Can you explain to me why you are disturbing my peace? Can you tell me why your mouth can't stay still?" But the words would not come out of my mouth.

"You know what they did to my first son?" the man asked me. "They shot him five times and left him to die in the ravine. So when my wife said that we should send Junior to England to study, I agreed. And now in London, they have stabbed him in the underground. It happened in the morning, when the train was full of commuters. No one stopped the attackers. The police say they are still studying the CCTV footage."

I had read in the papers of a Nigerian youth who had been stabbed on a train in London. So this was the father of the boy! I remembered the man's face then, his picture had been included in the report. His name was Mr Adeniji.

"I have spoken to many newspapers," the man said, "but

I want to take it further. I will go to NTA, DBN, AIT, every broadcasting station in Lagos. I will talk. Oh yes, I will go to the television stations and tell my country that nowhere is safe. I will go to Walter Carrington Crescent and tell all those queuing for British visas that there is no safety anywhere."

Nowhere is safe, I said to myself. *How very apt.* Once upon a time, Ibok was a safe and serene town. All had changed.

When I landed at Lagos airport, Boniface was not there to pick me up as agreed. I rang him.

"You lucky bastard!" Boniface shouted down the phone. "Tell me, how many girls did you have?"

"Stop that nonsense," I said. "You promised to pick me up at the airport. Where are you?"

Boniface muttered something about having a flat tyre. "I swear I wanted to come and pick you up, but this foolish car of mine disappointed me."

I should have known Boniface was unreliable. I hung up and walked towards the taxi rank, but it was one of those days that the spirit of the traffic jam had descended on the streets of Lagos; the spirit and its legions of confusion and disorder. If I took a car taxi, I could end up in traffic for many hours. I chose a motorcycle taxi.

"Oga, I beg, drive well," I told the motorcyclist.

If the man had heard me, he pretended not to. He squeezed through a narrow space between two jeeps. I closed my eyes. When I opened them again, we were on the wrong side of the road.

"You shouldn't do that," I screamed. But the man laughed and continued his crazy drive.

"Stop there!" A uniformed man jumped in front of the motorcycle. The machine screeched to a halt. Two other uniformed men appeared.

"Hand over the keys now!" the officer demanded.

"What is the meaning of this?" I asked as I struggled to get off the motorbike.

The uniformed officials turned to me. Their eyes took in my shoes, my wristwatch and luggage. In one glance they had sized me up. "You should be thankful we are not arresting you too," one of the men said.

"Me?" I asked.

"Yes, you."

"Arrest me for what?"

"For using the services of this motorbike," the man replied. "Don't you know that motorcycles are banned from plying their trade on this route?"

The government had recently announced that motorcycle taxis were banned from using some routes in the state, but the law had never been enforced. Everybody knew that.

"I saw two motorcycles speed past," I said. "Why didn't you stop them?"

"Oh, so you want to teach me my job, right?" the uniformed official snapped at me.

"I am just telling you the right thing," I responded.

The two other uniformed men stepped close to me. I could smell the men's breath. Something slightly overpowering, like garlic. "We have warned you to go away quietly," one of the men said.

"Why should you arrest this motorcycle rider, when others just sped past?" I asked.

The man raised his hands. "I have warned you enough..."

"If you touch me, I swear the whole of Lagos will hear about this," I threatened.

"And who are you?" the official sneered.

"I am a journalist."

The uniformed men stepped back. The one who had raised his hands to strike me sighed. He knew that I could expose them for hitting a civilian. And it could cost them their jobs.

"You should have told us you were a journalist," the man said. "I am a family man. I have seven kids and a wife who does not work. This is the only job that I am doing, the only one that brings food on my table. I don't want trouble, please. Mr Journalist, you and your motorcycle can go."

To make up for his failure to pick me at the airport, Boniface bought me lunch at The Lord Is My Shepherd Foods. To my amazement, the canteen had been given a facelift. New plastic chairs replaced the wooden benches and clean cloths, imported ones, adorned the tables. I was sad to notice that the waitresses still wore their oil-stained aprons.

"I want to hear about your escapades with the ladies," Boniface said. "Give it to me."

I stared at my food, and the kpomo in my plate stared back at me. I looked up and began to tell Boniface everything, filling in every detail: how I met Idara, how pretty she was, how I found her in the office having sex with a strange man.

Boniface shook his head. "A very sad story. What is paining me is that you didn't have a taste of her honey."

"I wanted everything to be perfect," I said. "I didn't want our relationship to be based on sex. Tell me, was I right to run away?"

"Of course, you were right," Boniface reassured me.

My mother was still asking me to reconsider. When I arrived at Lagos, she spent almost an hour on the phone, talking about how miserable Idara had become. "The girl really likes you," she said.

I thanked Boniface for lunch and then went to see my boss regarding feedback on the documentary script I gave him. Apollo Man shook his head vigorously as he said: "We cannot broadcast the programme. Let's pretend your trip did not happen. Do you hear?"

The words hit me like a hot slap. Perhaps I had not heard the man properly. "Sir?"

"It's not good for the government," the manager said. "Your documentary is too embarrassing. How could the events you report be believed now that everybody is lauding the amnesty programme?"

"That's the reason we should broadcast something on air!" I shouted out in exasperation. "We must expose them."

"Expose who? Ah, Ifiok, you are letting this thing get to you. You are being partial. That's not good. Remember, a journalist must report news stories objectively. He must put sentiments aside. He shouldn't take sides."

I was sure my ears were playing tricks on me. "We need to broadcast the programme, sir."

My boss looked up. "Didn't you hear me? I said we couldn't broadcast it. The matter is closed. Your work in the Niger Delta is complete."

"This is not right." I stood up to face him.

"Are you now teaching me how to do my job, eh?"

"Sir, I cannot let this happen."

"Have you forgotten who you are? Is something wrong with your head?"

I did not know where the boldness came from as I said, "Nothing is wrong with me, sir. I am just telling you that this is not right. It is so very wrong."

"Get out of my office!"

We faced each other. Apollo Man breathed heavily down

his nose. Then words came out of my own mouth before I could swallow them, "You are a chicken. You are scared of doing the right thing. You should be ashamed of yourself."

"That's it!" the manager screamed. "You are suspended. Get out of my office!"

Boniface was the first person to visit me at home. His car rattled to a stop beside the wobbly gate. He started screaming my name even before he got to my door.

"You, something is certainly wrong with your head," he told me, when I had let him in. "A nut is loose in your head. But I will find that missing nut myself and fix it. Yes, I will screw it tight." I said nothing. I didn't even welcome him properly.

"Have you ever heard of anyone talking back to any manager at work?" Boniface asked.

"Then let me be the first!" I shouted. "Let me be the first to tell him he's wrong."

"And you are happy with your result, eh? You are happy to be suspended, abi?"

"Sometimes, people have to show the way. The right way."

"And who are you to show the way? Are you God?"

"I am a journalist. So are you, Boniface. We are the custodians of our society. We are the gatekeepers of society. Have you forgotten the oath we took? The contracts we signed to uphold truth and defend values?"

Boniface smiled. "Those were just papers, my dear brother. Ordinary papers that meant nothing, that carried no weight. For God's sake, be real."

That was the whole idea, I told him calmly. I was being real. I had asked the manager to be real. To tell the world the truth, what they ought to know, what they deserved to know. "I will find that missing nut," Boniface promised. "I promise you that I will find it and fix it in your head."

I laughed. It was the first time that I had laughed in several hours. "There is no loose nut from my head. I am not a robot. I am a man of ideas. I am a man full of ideas. I am a virile man. Blood flows in my veins. The blood of justice."

"Let us not argue about right and wrong," Boniface begged. "The truth is not real when there is corruption. The truth is that you cannot fight a corrupt system. I cannot. None of us in the radio station can. The best thing to do now, Ifiok, is to go and beg the manager's forgiveness. Go with an elder, someone who can evoke sympathy. Tell him that you are sorry. Begging. That is what this country is all about. You can beg yourself out of the hangman's noose. Go and beg to be reinstated."

I refused to beg. The next day, I dusted off my CV and went to Ikoyi. I had heard that the famous Adeleke family was planning to open a radio station in Lagos; a radio station that would break down barriers and change the face of broadcasting in the country. I had not paid much attention to it before.

The building housing the head office of the company was situated in the heart of Ikoyi, just beside the newly redecorated park. Adeleke Investments branded itself as a responsible organisation, supporting a number of community programmes focused on education, particularly in villages.

"Please, can I see the human resources manager involved with the radio station?" I asked the receptionist.

There was no long procedure, no long application processes. The job had been advertised through word of mouth. Interested applicants arrived at the office and were taken to meet the manager.

"The manager is busy," the receptionist responded.

"I will wait," I said.

The receptionist shrugged while I sat down in the lobby and

picked up the company magazine. It was glossy, full colour. A message from the Chief Executive Officer of the company caught my attention: "As an international company, located in the heart of Lagos, with well-established links with companies abroad and a highly diverse staff body, we are already better-placed than most companies to ensure our customers come into contact with new products, cultures and ideas when they use our services. However, we want to do more and encourage our customers to expect more from us."

"The manager is free now," the receptionist announced two hours later.

I trudged along the polished corridors of the building. There were several pictures of the company's top executives on the walls. Most of them were women. All the pictures had short captions, but I didn't have the time to read them. The manager's office was next door to a meeting room. I knocked and entered.

"Hello, Ifiok," the manager greeted me, and I was surprised to see that it was Funke Adeleke, the lady I met on the plane a while ago. The same lady my cousin had brought to Ibok. We shook hands.

"Good to see you," I said.

"How is Ibok?" she asked. "I heard about the rise of violence there. It's sad, isn't it?"

"Very sad," I responded.

"We were just finalising plans to build our banks there before Ubong went into hiding."

Funke skimmed through my CV while we talked about trends in broadcasting, about the state radio stations, about the BBC African Performance that promoted African drama on the British station. I found myself remembering what Ubong had said about her honey pot.

"We have ambitious plans for this radio station," she revealed. "We will change the face and sound of broadcasting. Other radio stations will be envious of us. Our equipment will be arriving from China shortly. This is the time to join us." As she talked, it became apparent that she had much love for the new radio station and it pleased me.

"I am very excited about this radio station, Ifiok," the manager continued. "In fact, we will be broadcasting in the UK via satellite. We will give black Africans in the UK a voice."

"So when will the radio station start?" I asked.

The lady smiled. "Sometime next year. We have the license already and some of the equipment has arrived."

My heart sank. I would not be able to survive for that long without a job. From then on, my mind kept going back and forth between the exciting idea of the radio station and how long it would take before I could be paid to work for it. Funke promised to stay in touch. I thanked the lady and left.

Chapter 30

Boniface's uncle and auntie pleaded with Apollo Man on my behalf. They arrived at the radio station in a battered blue van just after noon. I had rented the vehicle from Sammy, my neighbour who ran a car hire business to augment his civil service pay. But my rented crowd had to wait for an hour because the manager was in a meeting with auditors from Abuja.

At exactly half past one, the manager appeared and took them inside his office. I hovered outside until I was called in.

"Ifiok is like a son to me," Boniface's uncle began. "He is nothing at all like some other young people that I have known. I am talking about a man who pays respect. Whenever he sees me, he greets me in the proper manner, the Yoruba way, even though he is not Yoruba. This boy is a good boy from a good home."

I could not look at the manager's face. If the walls could talk, would they tell Apollo Man that everything Boniface's uncle said was a lie?

"Ifiok has a good heart," the man continued. "I look after him like my biological son. Since his parents are not here in this town, I am his father. So I come here today as his father."

The manager coughed and I looked up. I thought the man was going to say something, but he didn't utter a word.

"Manager, I want you to forgive this boy," the uncle begged.

"Pardon him. He is a small boy."

When the manager eventually spoke, his voice sounded tired. "This is not about being a good boy or not," he said. "This is about responsibility, about respect, about rules in the workplace."

"I agree," Boniface's uncle said. "I know about respect. Did I not just tell you that this boy is full of respect? But sometimes things happen. Things happen that make them show us that they are still boys."

The manager said that the case had reached the director's desk. The administration manager had taken a special interest in the matter. "So you see, the case is beyond me," he said. "Now that people more powerful are involved, it has become difficult."

Boniface's uncle smiled. "Nothing is too difficult for us. Not in this country, anyway."

They had come prepared. The man brought out a bottle of wine that I had purchased the day before. It was the manager's favourite drink. I watched as my boss' face lit up.

"We have come to plead," the uncle said, "to make peace, to bury the past and move forward. Please forgive him for whatever foolish thing he did."

At that moment, just as we had planned it, I went down on my knees. "Forgive me, sir. I was foolish. I acted foolishly. Please, take me back."

I was taken back.

As usual at lunch time, The Lord Is my Shepherd Foods was filled with hungry mouths when I went for a meal. A new waitress who, thank goodness, wore a clean apron took my order. Waiting for my food, I looked around at the faces that were bent over their plates. At my table, two men were arguing about their neighbour at home. Across from them, a young lady was cracking a chicken bone. Most of the customers wore long faces. It was understandable. These were civil servants whose wage was too meagre to take home. They had to devise other means to increase their incomes, from accepting bribe to direct selling.

"Sir, your food," the waitress said as she brought my order.

I poked at the fish on my plate. Poor fish! When it came into this world, did it know that someday it would make that sad journey from the belly of the sea to the belly of a hungry human?

"Ifiok, there you are!" Boniface shouted as he walked towards me. "I have been looking all over the place for you."

"What it is it?" I asked.

Boniface pulled up a chair. "Please, don't give me that look. Are you mourning someone? No. So why don't you eat your food and be happy that you have life?"

I stared at my colleague. Then I stared at my food. A song about life and death began to croak out of the loudspeakers in the canteen.

"Please, don't let that good food go to waste," Boniface told me. "You have a job. You have food and you are able to eat. So what is your problem?"

I picked my cutlery. Boniface was right, I had life. What more could I want?

"Tune the TV to AIT!" someone demanded suddenly. "There's breaking news!"

A waiter tuned into the station. "Breaking News" in a banner headed the screen. The presenter announced that the Ibok Youth Movement had bombed a major oil installation in Ibok. I sat up. Some youths were speaking to the camera. A close-up shot revealed that they were the students of the film class.

"This is just the beginning!" Nsima screamed. "Let the government and the corporations be warned. We are going to bomb three more installations and the government offices if the politicians do not listen to us. We demand that they keep their promises."

My desire to eat had gone.

Acknowledgements

I thank the following people for their support and encouragement: the Society of Authors' Authors' Foundation, Tony Elumelu, Louise South, Emem Isong, Uduak Isong, Chidi Oguamanam, Ayo Ojebode, James Attah, Kunle Shittu, Richard Adetula, Noma Moyo, Kachi Ozumba, Jude Dibia, Father Abraham Jatto, Basil Enoch, Akan Ukpong, Sue Thomas, Alex Evans. I would also like to thank the team at Jacaranda Books, especially my editors Valerie Brandes and Laure Deprez.

About the Author

Anietie Isong has won several writing prizes including the Commonwealth Short Story Award and the inaugural Olaudah Equiano Prize for Fiction. In 2009, his short story *Devotion* was selected as one of the exciting new stories from the next generation of English short story writers and published in the anthology *Roads Ahead*, edited by Catherine O'Flynn. Anietie studied at the University of Ibadan and the University of Leicester. *Radio Sunrise* is his first novel.